ALONE.

ALONE.

Michael Califra

Hadrian Paperbacks

NEW YORK

First Hadrian printing 2020

ISBN: 978-0-578-65292-4

Library of Congress Control Number: 2020905249

Cover photo by M-C Brulé

10 9 8 7 6 5 4 3 2 1

ALONE.

I HAD BEAUTIFUL EYES. When I was young everyone told me so.

Enlarged in the makeup mirror they seemed smaller now, more deeply set in their sockets, their brightness dimmed by decades of life. Lines at the outer edges, described as "crow's feet" early in middle age and owned proudly as a sign of her increasing maturity, were now fleshy folds of skin. Only when gently pulled back with her fingertip did they resemble what the slippage of time had altered so unrelentingly.

Glancing up, the entirety of the ageing, sixty-seven-year-old face stared back from the mirror on the medicine cabinet. Paige, when did this happen to you? Beautiful in her youth, she was unquestionably an attractive woman, even in her later years, but could not fathom how so much time could have passed so quickly; decades that had left their mark on her: the puffy morning bags under her eyes; the many tiny, vertical crevices that appeared on her mouth when she pursed her lips; the sagging skin on her neck and throat. Through the open door, the reflection also betrayed the unmade, rumpled bed; evidence, not only of another night of restless anxiety, but of the vacant space that was Henry's. The aching sensation of irreversible loss, one of the few true sensations Paige was still capable of feeling, returned. It was just after six in the morning. Better, she thought, than four or five when darkness still enveloped the house. For weeks after Henry's death, she had been suddenly woken at those hours by a profound sense of dread that invaded her body like a chill.

Wrapped in her bathrobe, Paige went downstairs to the kitchen and made coffee. Just four scoops now, she thought, reminding herself yet again. Staring at the gurgling coffeemaker, the numbness of being a single entity in the world was palpable, even if somewhat less intense than it had been even a couple of weeks ago. Like a recent amputee experiencing the shock of losing part of herself, she was slowly coming to terms with the reality of the missing limb, even if, at times, she unconsciously assumed it was still present, only to be cruelly slammed by reality while performing a simple act. Just four scoops now. 'I miss Henry,' she mumbled. For years, she would be the first one up and in the kitchen, making coffee for two. Eight to ten scoops instead of the four she now used. She poured the coffee into the mug and added the milk, now well past its *sell by* date, relived that it had not betrayed her by showing itself gone sour. Paige took the coffee out onto the back porch. Again, she took note of the small, wood trim under the screen door, which Henry had such difficulty surmounting in his last days. Sixteen years her senior, she had, in the course of their forty years together, seen him go from youthful and dashing, to handsome middle age, elderly, and, finally, invalid. It was now forty-four hollow days since Henry had died. There had been a constant parade of people visiting her in the days that followed, often bearing food. Food, she thought; as if I am incapable of driving ten minutes to the supermarket, or preparing it myself. It was as though she was now assumed to be the invalid in this house; the amputee invalid with a part missing. There were also the phone calls. She could count on the phone ringing at around ten in the morning and continuing sporadically throughout the day until eight or nine in the evening. People calling to see how she was. *How are you doing, Paige?* How am I doing? How do they think I'm doing? Henry isn't here. I still am. Maybe that's what they really want to know – whether I'm still here. In a couple of weeks' time, the visits and food slowed and the calls became less frequent until they had ceased. Friends and neighbors had paid their respects. They had done their duty and now had moved on from their concern and back into daily routines, removed from her grief and mourning. Paige sat on the back porch in solitude. Alone.

. . .

The wind rustles the gray birch trees in the yard like spirits, she remembered telling someone soon after she and Henry had moved into the house; a place she loved from the first moment she saw it. In what would be their last sitting together on the porch, Paige and Henry had talked about how tall those trees, which were little more than saplings when they moved in, had become in the intervening years. Henry had guessed their height to be forty feet. It was just weeks ago. Paige recalled the heartbreak she felt, watching Henry's arm shaking as he brought the mug of coffee to his quivering lips; so much so that he needed to use two hands. That was during warm summer, and still, Henry needed to be wrapped in multiple layers to avoid feeling cold. Now it was past peak foliage. The spirits were busy tearing the leaves from their branches. Soon the trees would be bare, crooked skeletons through which those spirits sometimes howled, as if to mock the living. The peeling, white paint on the wooden railing brought back recollections of how shabby the house was when they bought it decades ago.

Back then, Paige found its unkempt condition part of the house's charm. How young she was when they moved here. Paige could see the previous owner in her mind; a widow she had thought elderly, but who was probably no older back then than she was now, and quite possibly younger. Eventually, when the house's 'charm' became water leaks of various kinds, and the rotted wood around the windows allowed the drafty apparitions outside to take over the house with a growing ferocity, their slow but steady renovations over the years made it pristine. Now it had become somewhat shabby again. Paige thought that houses often reflected the lives of their inhabitants in that way. She and Henry had both loved the covered back porch. It was the main reason they bought the house, despite it not being in the best of repair. It was here that they had some of their most satisfying conversations over breakfast when the weather permitted. And it was rare that it didn't, even if for many of their younger years, an electric heater had to be employed to make it tolerable. Unlike other couples their age who, more often than not, spent their time together in depleted silence, they were not talked out. Henry always had something interesting to say. Even with age advancing, and as he withdrew from the city, preferring to stay secluded in the house and its immediate surroundings, the more he used that time to read every newspaper and magazine he could find, in print or online. They would talk about music, art, politics, the neighbors, themselves, and sometimes mortality. Both were committed atheists; Henry even more committed than she was. While Paige had no use for the tenets of organized religion, regarding them all as fairy tales, she always left the door open to some kind of afterlife, or reincarnation, or slip into another dimension, or whatever, because, after all, who really knew? Even a brainy fellow like Einstein had thought it possible through the science of physics. Henry, on the other hand, was resolute about going into the ground, or up in smoke, and nowhere else. At times Paige thought Henry used his views on the matter only to present a masculine fearlessness. No matter what his beliefs, or fears, might have actually been, now he has found out, she thought, and feelings of abandonment emerged again in her. Paige had been left behind. No matter what death turned out to be, it held no fear for her any longer. It had already happened to Henry so she had nothing to fear. The thought of survival alone is what filled her with dread. At the very end of Henry's life, bedridden and sedated to unconsciousness, drawing quick, shallow breaths, Paige sat at his bedside holding his hand. The peculiar odor that the hospice nurse said was the result of the body shutting down, would suddenly invade her senses at odd times over the last weeks. Could that have been Henry signaling he was here? Or just the powerful organ known as the brain unleashing evolution's way of coping with loss. She preferred to believe the former, wondering how Henry would rationalize, or regret, having disapproved of such notions so strongly now that he might be trying to signal her from wherever he might be.

The hot coffee drunk, Paige saw her neighbor, Charlotte, walking in her backyard, which bordered her own, stopping to pick up something near the fence. When Charlotte noticed Paige she clutched her heart with both hands; a sign of love and caring for her neighbor of decades. Paige smiled and waved as if from an island; quarantined from the rest of humanity by her recent loss. By the unique universality of her loss. One of Charlotte's teenage grandsons ran to her, and the two walked back to the house, leaving Paige alone once again. Paige and Charlotte were roughly the same age. She had lost her husband several years before Henry died. Something about what Paige had just witnessed sent a sensation of uneasiness running through her. She went back into the house and sat in the living room, observing the baby-grand piano. Henry was an accomplished jazz pianist; Paige had been classically trained. For all of their lives, separately and together, the piano and the music it produced were an all-consuming passion. She had not once touched the keys since Henry had died, and even in the weeks before his death, only for a few minutes now and then to relieve the tension she felt during the last stages of his illness. It occurred to her that this was the longest stretch of not playing since she had first touched a keyboard as a young girl. School work was mechanical and passionless. Something that she was indifferent to; a requirement that had to be met to the satisfaction of her parents and teachers. There had never been any desire on her part to outperform; to do more beyond what was necessary to be respectable. Nor did any of the subjects bring any real satisfaction. Not like the piano did. None required the dexterity in her fingers that amazed people, or made them come alive. None produced the effusive praise about her talent she overheard friends and relatives offering her mother. From the very first time she lifted the fallboard of her first piano she had always been reluctant to close it again. Now, for the first time since she had discovered it, that passion was gone.

Paige sat on the sofa, switched on the television and watched cable-news talking heads discussing the latest outrage; the seemingly unstable president and his angry *Tweets*. Paige had only a vague notion of the social medium or how it worked, but sensed, as with so much lately, that the world had been a better place without it. Tweets aside, she and Henry had been equally aghast at the state of affairs in Washington over the past couple of years, and recalled him often saying, 'Just when you think it can't possibly get worse it always does.' The television could not hold her attention, however. Not many things could in the state of constant, vague agitation she had been experiencing for weeks now. Repetitive and unchanging, she felt she could tune out the news for months and pick it up right where she left off simply by switching the set back on. No matter how big and egregious the news of the day might be, it now seemed distant, and could not in any way compare to the bereavement she carried constantly within her. Surveying the living room, she felt a rush of memories that had been held in check by the overwhelming events of Henry's deepening illness, sudden absence, and the flurry of activity that followed it: all the loose ends that needed to be tied following the death of a person; the people who had to be dealt with, many of whom were friends who thought they were doing good, but in reality only added to her burden. She could now remember what had long been forgotten or simply became assigned to the deeper recesses of the mind. Observing the piano, Paige recalled how she and Henry often sat side by side on the bench while the other played, critiquing one another's technique, or just having fun playing duets while enjoying a bottle of wine, or even two. In the early years in the house, touching of hands, accidentally or intentionally, or the sensual pressing of shoulders, could lead to passionate love on the floor right where she was now sitting. So many other spaces in the house contained intense memories of joy and love, or sadness and anger. She became aware, for the first time, that the photos displayed of the two of them around the corner of the living room were photos of them separately. How did it happen that there weren't photos of them together? Certainly, there were many taken over the years. The only framed connection between the two of them was a portrait that Henry had painted of her when she was in her mid-twenties. The piano had belonged to them both. The oils, brushes and canvases in the attic, which Henry used as an art studio, were exclusively his. Unlike the clothing, still hanging in Henry's closet, and now seemed simply ownerless, the artist's paraphernalia, instruments of Henry's creative expression, now expressed the disconsolate loneliness of the orphaned. So heart-wrenching had Paige found the sight of the studio with Henry gone that she hadn't had the stomach to open the door to it more than once since his death.

The warm shower hitting her back felt like a body massage; an approximation of intimate, loving human contact, which Paige now thought forever lost and beyond her reach. She indulged herself in it for a good long time. It had been several days since she had bathed. Today Paige thought she would make a quick trip to the local market and pick up a few things like milk and bread. Coffee was also in short supply, as were eggs. She had put off going into town simply because she had no desire to hear yet more condolence talk from anyone she might happen meet there. She had already had her fill of it and did not want to hear more. Nor did she want invitations to visit people who thought it sad that she was now spending her days alone. She much preferred being alone with her memories than to be pressed into arduous, pointless small talk with people who really never meant all that much to her. Being in the house alone was at times painful, but the pain was hers. It would be there no matter how often people told her what a wonderful man Henry was or how much they miss him. They hardly knew him, anyway. Not the way she did. And what did they know about her loneliness? She had to endure that first night alone in the bed she had shared with Henry, knowing he would never return. That's when you know what it is to be alone.

Dressed in sweatpants and sweatshirt, she proceeded down the staircase to the main floor of the house. The narrow staircase was a space in which she had, long ago, envisioned jostling past a couple of rampaging children. Henry wanted no children, however. So, in time, she sacrificed her desire to him, leaving her 'husband' the only one to collide against on those frenetic mornings when both were late for one thing or another. Those things, once so all-consuming and important, now meant so little that she could not even imagine what they might have been. Yet, one 'what might have been,' her childlessness, remained. For the first time since Henry died, she felt a deep resentment toward him. By now, she should have been jostling past grandchildren on that staircase. How wonderful that now seemed.

There should have been grown children of her own visiting her, calling her, making sure she was all right and not so alone. Her own flesh and blood mixed with Henry's. The only people in the world who really mattered. The only people whose concern for her now would have been genuine, and without an expiration date. There should have been at least one. There would have been at least one if it were not for Henry's horror at her accidental pregnancy, which Paige could finally admit was not accidental at all. At least not as she remembered it now. Why did she let him push her into aborting it? She could not remember why she did. She only remembered that he was relentless about it. Henry was relentless about everything he wanted. But she, too, was complicit and she knew it. She was an artist. Her music had to come first. Faced with the impending, real-life prospect of making it second to raising a child, she relented. Others could populate the world with offspring; she would help uplift it with her gift. There would be time for a child later; after some undefined professional goal had been met. She had thought time existed in abundance, not realizing how precious or fleeting each day was. Back then, even when the days and weeks seemed to pass quickly, there was the understanding that there were always much more ahead. That was how she rationalized acquiescing to Henry's incessant, room-to-room hounding that she terminate the pregnancy. And she did have a gift. Everyone said it, even before she met Henry. But he cultivated it in new ways with the lessons he gave her. He became her teacher. He taught her improvisation, which he always said was more difficult to master than even the most complex classical pieces. Paige was young and impressionable then. She looked up to him. From the very first time Paige heard him play she was captivated by the colors he gave to his jazz improvisations. His playing reminded her of Bill Evans. She told him that the very first night she saw him perform with his trio at a jazz club in their native Chicago. He did not even feign interest when he off handedly replied, 'Lady, I passed that phase a long time ago' and walked away, leaving Paige stunned and embarrassed. Henry was vain and intense. When he took a break during his gigs, he would disappear to the coat-check room with a book and read, avoiding contact with people, even his own sax and bass players. Yet Paige was immediately attracted to him. She was twenty-three and engaged; Henry was thirty-nine and married. It was her fiancé, George Haskell, who had brought her to the club that night. He had seen Henry play there previously and wanted Paige to hear him, too. When George asked what she thought, Paige said that she thought Henry was an arrogant asshole. George agreed, but said that, luckily, they didn't have to live with him, just enjoy his music.

Paige's sudden recollection of how effortlessly she terminated her engagement to George startled her. She had not thought about it in decades, and even then only in passing as something she could not help and was not responsible for. How could she have been so cold? It was so unlike her. She had always thought of herself as a warm person. Henry thought of her as a warm soul. Yet she so easily devastated George. George, who was a good man and did everything in his power to make her happy, purely out of his love for her. But Henry's mysterious pull on Paige was strong. She began showing up on her own at the club he played at; the one George had brought her to, to see the man he certainly went out of his way to find because he knew Paige would enjoy hearing him and watching him play. For reasons she could not understand, she felt pangs of guilt; guilt she had never felt before over treating George the way she had more then forty years ago. How, when she told him their relationship was over, she turned a callous, deaf ear to George's pleas; his many tearful declarations of undying love; his desire to have children with her and only her, tragically unaware of how pathetic all of it seemed to Paige since she had become so enamored of Henry. A situation George was only too aware of having brought on himself by bringing her to the club in the first place. Paige could not understand why her thoughts had turned to George so often since Henry died. She felt hurt by the fact that he hadn't called her. Even after she had left him, Paige and George had remained friends, solely by virtue of George's bottomless ability to endure the emotional pain she had heaped on him, until becoming seemingly numb to it, just so he, as he told her once, might continue to have her in his life. Henry tolerated George; his occasional telephone calls, and even his meeting Paige from time to time for dinner or a show in the city when he was in town on business. Henry was supremely confident in his hold on Paige and had never shown any sign of jealousy or insecurity when she occasionally went out with other male friends; even when she didn't call him from the city apartment before going to bed, or had arrived back at the house upstate in the wee hours. Even when Paige sometimes subtly tried to ignite some jealousy in Henry, she never could. From midlife through to his end, she felt that Henry took her for granted. Only after an argument brought on by Henry's stubbornness could she manage to extract a confession from Henry that she had indeed brought joy into his life.

It was now nearly ten o'clock. Feeling pangs of hunger, Paige went to the kitchen and made breakfast. For a good while after Henry's death she had felt no need to eat anything at all. Hunger had become lost to her, not just in regard to food, but for anything except air and water and coffee. She had been reduced to a mere existence of sorrow. Yet, little by little, owing to the body's innate pursuit of self-preservation, the need for solid food had returned to her. Not that she could ever imagine wanting to defrost one of the three pans of lasagna sitting rock-solid in her freezer. Three different people had labored to produce them thinking they were doing something good and noble, but what could ever make a person think lasagna could ease her mourning in any way? Two were in tin pans but one was in a glass baking dish, which would have to be returned eventually. But to whom? So much of the past few weeks was a blur; she had no idea who had given it to her. That one, the one in the glass baking dish, produced feelings of bitterness in Paige. Two scrambled eggs would suffice, just as they had yesterday, and the day before that, thank you very much. And two were all that was left. Paige put on another four-scoop pot of coffee. Though she had always been the first down to the kitchen, Henry would soon join her there. From the open kitchen, which looked out into the living room, Paige stared at the staircase. She could almost hear his slow, heavy, early-morning footsteps descending them as she had heard them countless times over the years before seeing him emerge at the bottom of the stairs, wrapped in his bathrobe, grasping the banister, still groggy. He would kiss her cheek, as Paige stood at the coffee maker and ask her preference: pancakes? Eggs? French Toast? as he opened the pantry doors. Henry was a surprisingly good cook. He would usually make breakfast and often dinner. Now Paige prepared the eggs herself in a kitchen that, for a time, seemed larger without Henry, but now just painfully vacant. Rinsing and wiping with a sponge, first a plate and then the small bowl taken from the sink in which she had beaten eggs yesterday, Paige cracked open the shells and dropped the contents into it. She rinsed the whisk still in the sink and beat them; scraped the iron skillet of yesterday's dried, yellow egg with the spatula, rinsed it, and heated it on the stove. Taking butter from the refrigerator, she cut a slice with the last clean knife from the kitchen drawer, flicking it into the pan before relegating it to the sink next all the other knives she had previously used. She watched the butter melt sufficiently on the warming skillet's surface, and poured in the eggs. Realizing she had forgotten to clean the spatula, Paige quickly scratched the dried, yellow residue off its leading edge with her fingernail and wiped it off with a towel. She began pulling, lifting and folding the eggs again and again until they were done, more or less, to her satisfaction. Utensils recycled straight from the sink were returned to it. All her movements required minimal effort. The eggs would taste exactly as they had yesterday. As they would taste tomorrow. This is how my life will be from now on. Flatlined. No reason or desire for anything to be different. Days as numb as I'm feeling inside, passing one by one. Base needs met. Nothing more needed or wanted. Nothing more is possible. Days to muddle through with obligations to be fulfilled, because everyone expects them to be. Because not fulfilling them would bring unpleasantness from authorities. If one is still among the living, there are requirements to be met, no matter how empty or lonely that life has become. Paige took the eggs, along with the mug of coffee, out to the back porch. Wind had started kicking up; a thick layer of gray, curdled cloud was moving in. A storm was coming. If she had listened to the radio she would have heard the weather forecast. She would always switch the radio on in the kitchen in the morning. Now she didn't want the noise: the loud commercials, the upbeat, fast talking voices trying to convince people to get up and out into this new day, as if it were full of promise and new opportunity for all. It wasn't a new day for Paige. It was the past and the future. It didn't much matter what the weather would be like. She thought again about going to the market. During her last trip there more a week ago, she had enjoyed the respite from being in the house alone. Driving over the curving and turning back roads she knew so well felt good. Henry always nagged her about driving too fast, and maybe he was right. 'You're gonna kill us both!' she remembered him often shouting. Now she drove however she wanted to. She was in absolute control. It was her first taste of freedom; her first sense of having a new life ahead as open as the road before her. Liberation. At the same time, she remembered Henry's dry humor; the deadpan way he'd say that he would warn the neighbors to stay off the street whenever Paige announced that she was taking a drive to the market, and her grief retuned. The respite was an illusion. Paige didn't want freedom. She wanted Henry. Taking the same trip again today would not produce that feeling of liberation, but only of emptiness. During her last visit to the market Paige had run into Katherine Bonclair, who offered condolences and told Paige how her son, Barry, who had just graduated from college, was heartbroken when she told him Henry had passed. Barry had still fondly recalled Henry's *Jazz-a-matazz* visits to his school. Henry always thought that music education should start as early as possible — in elementary schools, not just in middle school. He developed a program and went from one school to another a couple of times a year, letting young pupils see and hear various musical instruments, letting the children touch and play them, and by the end of each session he had organized them into a band in which everyone played several notes in some loud, discombobulation of a tune. The kids loved it; *Jazz-a-matazz* became sought after every year with Henry often getting marvelous press from it. He pretended not to care, and even feigned annoyance with those small articles and the accompanying photos that would sometimes appear in the local paper.

But Paige knew the recognition meant something to him. She had always been proud when she read them. Thinking about them now, however, saddened her. How insignificant the praise had become for an artist so gifted. How small the man, who had once harbored such grand aspirations, had wound up.

The solitude of her late breakfast on the porch was interrupted when the phone rang. It had been two days since anyone had called. Paige was surprised by the excitement the ringing telephone had stirred in her. And by the disappointment when it turned out to be a mortgage broker who, in a voice as solemn as it was disingenuous, said that he knew Paige had suffered a terrible loss recently and wondered if refinancing at a lower rate might be in order – just for peace of mind. Paige simply hung up, not so much out of anger as bemusement. She thought of the conversation she'd had with the young voice at the funeral home when she called to make arrangements for Henry. How he told her he had a 'deal' for her, asking at the end of the conversation, 'Well, can we do this?' She felt as though he was trying to sell her a used car. When did even bereavement become so blatantly a business opportunity? One of the reasons they had moved to the village of Staatsburg was because it was genuine. It had given them a reprieve from the constant hustling and pretense of New York City. In nearby Woodstock there was an artists' community begun in the 1920s. Close by in Rhinebeck there were restaurants and galleries. It was their retreat. It gave them the opportunity to be who they were. Now, even their private corner of the world had been polluted by greedy commerce. It saddened her. Too much seemed to be changing, all at the same time. Yet, while Paige had been enjoying her isolation in the house over the past couple of months, she knew that soon she would be forced from it. Henry had left a small life insurance policy, but the day was coming that she would be forced back to work. Back to the small rent-controlled apartment that Henry had gotten through convoluted means when they had first come to New York in the 1970s and such things were still possible. Back to the endless go of running from one piano student to another, sometimes five or six a day, and then a gig in the evening that would last until one in the morning or even later. She had been the breadwinner. It had been many years since Henry had earned any kind of income aside from his Social Security, which paid the mortgage on the house and a few ancillary expenses. For nearly twenty years Paige had reigned six nights a week over 'her room' at the Metropolitan Hotel; it had belonged to her as surely as the Café Carlyle had belonged to Bobby Short. Six years ago the hotel was bought by an Indian concern that wanted a 'new look' for the stately, old room. That's when her schedule became a hectic fight for survival, and the house an even more appreciated refuge. Henry had long since stopped visiting the city at that point. The older he had gotten the more he hated the crowds and the hassle of commuting. In the early years, even after they had bought the house, Henry would often accompany Paige to the city. They would breakfast late at the neighborhood diner; see an afternoon movie, or attend a museum exhibit before she would go to work at the hotel. Sometimes Henry would accompany her there, and he would also perform; an extra treat for her devotees. Those were the best years as far as Paige was concerned, though they now seemed so long ago, and so disconnected from her recent past that they may have been someone else's life involving someone other than Henry. The plate, now cleared of scrambled egg, along with the utensils used to consume them, were returned to the kitchen sink.

The old steamer trunk was a time machine, Paige thought, not just because of the memories it had contained in the form of photos, old letters and other artifacts of their lives together; but that she had been rummaging through it, dream-like and nostalgic, for nearly two hours before realizing how much time had passed. Knowing it was there, sitting dust-covered and Sphinx-like in the attic, she hadn't dedicated a thought to it in years. It had been relegated to the attic so it would be out of the way precisely because it had become too tiresome to look at. With a sudden need for tangible relics of her life with Henry, Paige had, from one moment to the next, suddenly become aware of it again and was drawn to it. The trunk itself was a relic, with its stickers from various steamship lines, leather straps and old, brass key locks. She and Henry had bought it at a local yard sale soon after moving into the house with the intention of using it as a coffee table, which it had been for many years before being hauled with great effort into the section of the attic used for storage. It had been such a long time since Paige had opened it that she'd forgotten much of its contents had even existed. She was astounded at how much it contained, crammed-full as it was with the minutiae of their lives; so much so that a lesser vessel would have burst at the seams. Paige wondered how it all came to be stored in it; she had only a vague recollection of putting a few things inside, mostly things that would be needed only when entertaining. None of those things were now there. In their place were pressed envelopes containing letters from her mother, clearly lonely and missing Paige, asking her to call more often and to perhaps think about visiting with Henry. Yet it was the old tour guide of Florence, Italy, that she found heartbreaking. There was a time when she and Henry imagined strolling the endlessly fascinating streets of that city. Henry used to talk about the Uffizi Gallery intimately, as though he had been there many times. The guide book was from 1983. They, or at least she, was certain they would make it there one day. Time seemed to be on their side until the years simply evaporated. Now Henry was dead. How many things they had planned to do together that never came to pass, and now never would. So many missed opportunities, she thought. Why hadn't they seized any of them when they had the chance? How did it happen that they never experienced the many things they had planned? She and Henry had been together nearly four decades. Why did it seem now that she was looking back on so much empty space? She had always thought they had lived a full life together. Now she saw that it was lived only partly; that much more had been possible. The allure of Henry was that she believed he offered a fuller life than George Haskell ever could have. Now she was sixty-seven years old, alone, and had never been to Florence. She wondered if George ever had been there. She knew he had been to Europe many times, both on business and with his late wife and their children. Paige made the determination that of course he had been. He still lived in the environs of Chicago, not far from where they had grown up, but she found it inconceivable that he had not been to Italy and Florence. A sense of irony overcame her, and she wondered again why George had been in her thoughts so much lately. She had not seen him in four or five years, and had not heard from him in at least. . . she tried to recall and thought that it had been at least three. She did remember that the last time he called was when his wife had died. Paige expressed her condolences, but didn't feel much empathy, eventually making an excuse to get off the phone because Henry wanted her attention; attention for what she no longer remembered, but she surrendered to him willingly, even as George was weeping in grief. Immediately after hanging up she had wondered why George felt the need to call her at all. As far as Paige was concerned, their relationship had been less than superficial for many, many years, which was why she could not explain the sense of longing she had been feeling for him over the last couple of weeks.

Paige reached for the coffee mug on the floor next to her. Realizing it was empty she went downstairs to make more. She stood at the kitchen counter, yet again listening to the percolating coffee machine, wondering what George's reaction would be if she called him. She did not know the last time she had done that. Probably not since she had left him for Henry. He had always called her, even after he had gotten married. Whenever he would be in New York she would get a phone call and he would ask if she would like to meet somewhere for dinner. Usually Paige said yes, probably out of some sense of pity, though she never really wanted to, and never particularly looked forward to meeting him. But George, unlike many of the wolves who came to the hotel to hear her play, was sweet and harmless. He would spend his hard-earned money, buying her a meal at a nice restaurant when she had the night off from her gig at the hotel and was still in the city. He would talk about his family. With those dinners over the years, George had chronicled his wedding and honeymoon; the birth of his two sons; family vacations; the kids' schooling through college, and the marriage of one of them. All this Paige knew for no other reason other than George wanting to share it with her; thinking that it mattered to her when in fact it did not. He would show her photos of his granddaughter, which only produced resentful feelings of envy in Paige, causing her to barely glance at them in an exhibition of obvious disinterest. It occurred to her that the act of calling him now would be a selfish one after the way she had felt about him all those years. Then a terrible thought: what if George had also died? He would be at least seventy years old now; the age where anything can happen to one's health. What are we but consciousness dependent on a collection of billions and billions of cells, any one of which could go berserk at any time causing a cascade leading to illness, suffering and death? We all are in possession of a genetic code inherited through countless generations. A defect in any gene passed down from a distant, unknown relative could do one in. The likelihood of it happening only increased with age. Henry had died from a collection of many things, any one, two or three of which would have been survivable. But the attack of all of them together weakened him, sending him into a long terminal decline. If George had indeed passed away she would probably not have heard about it. There was no one in Chicago she knew anymore. She had lost all contact to the place. Paige again thought that calling him now would be completely self-serving; a way to ease her loneness. And what if she did call, only to find the number had been disconnected; the same number she had had for him for decades? That would be an additional heartbreak. She seemed to recall some major health issue he was dealing with, but could not remember exactly what it was. Simply because she didn't care enough to listen when he talked about it during one of his calls. Was it cancer? Pancreatic cancer? Or was it prostate? If it was the first, he'd probably be gone. The latter offered more hope. She felt certain now that George must have died. It was the only reason that would account for his silence. The empty silence of the dead. Another who had left her alone. And why would she want to harbor any hope that he was still alive? She had had enough of that over last couple of years with Henry — hope for recoveries on days he seemed to rally; hopes that were always dashed when he relapsed. By not calling George, at least she would never know for sure. It had nothing to do with hope, but simple doubt. There could be some doubt in her mind if doubt was what it took to soothe her. Not calling would also be self-serving, but at least it would not be additionally painful. Nor would she have to deal with the guilt that would arise because of the way she had treated him over the years if she had found out that he was indeed dead.

Returning from her detour into George's fate, Paige realized that the coffee that she had gone to the kitchen to make was ready. She poured it into the mug, added milk, again relieved that it had not soured on her, and retreated to the living room. She stopped at the piano, regarding it with the sense of pity one would feel toward an ignored puppy, before finally sitting down before it. As she lifted the fallboard and spread her fingers on the keys, a wave of sadness washed over her. The musical notes, any combination of them, whether fully formed and structured or just in a rambling jumble had always invaded Paige and Henry's essence. No matter their proximity to each other, no matter what they had been doing, the musical notes produced by one or the other transcended the physical space in the house, bringing them together either to critique or to praise; enticing their intellect and passion as if in a grand seduction of their minds and souls. Paige found that she could not force a single note from the keyboard. She could not bear to hear the instrument emit any sound. Covering the keys again, she placed her hands gently upon the polished wood, preferring the company of the old steamer trunk and the memories held within it.

Sitting on the dusty hardwood floor, she struggled to pull out a heavy manila envelope, freeing it from the tightly-packed collection of things. Photographs of various sizes cascaded out if it and onto the floor as she accidentally held the wrong side up. Here were the photographs of Henry and Paige together: on an unidentified street in Chicago; at the Grand Canyon; sitting together in various rooms, and with people, many of whom she could not identify with any certainty; snapshots of the two of them at the piano at the hotel, and together and separately at other pianos in other places she no longer knew; at a long table in a restaurant surrounded by smiling faces. How young they both seemed. How attractive they were; the center of attention wherever they went. The photos were like 1950s paparazzi stills and the two of them were the glamorous stars. This was how she wanted to remember her life with Henry. Paige felt the blood rush happily to her head as she flipped through the photos one after another, as if they were a deck of cards, studying the faces in them. How could she have possibly thought they had wasted their time together? No one gets to do everything they planned to. Everyone has regrets; it's all part of life. But few had had the kind of life they did. Look at the dresses she'd had; the suits Henry wore. They seemed to radiate confidence. How slender and graceful; so lovely and smart. Yes, youth does that. Now she was holding the evidence that they had taken full advantage of it while it was theirs.

Again, the time machine had taken hold. Paige eventually felt deep pangs of hunger; the first time she had felt a genuine appetite since Henry had died. The envelope full of photos in hand, Paige was buoyant; she felt as if she were floating down the staircase to the kitchen with the risers pushing upward to meet each step. There was almost nothing left in the fridge; nothing that could come close to satisfying her. It was time to take a pan of lasagna out of its deep freeze; first a thaw in the microwave then a gentle reheating in the oven, the intervening time spent immersed in the time-lapse the photos had conjured. So many faces. So many friends. What could have become of them all? When the lasagna was done, Paige took a large plate of it out onto the porch. A new, clean plate this time with fresh utensils from the drawer. It was as if she was actually tasting the food on her plate for the first time in months. It was delicious. No longer a burden, she would have to make an effort, she thought, to find out who prepared and brought it to her. What a kind thing to do! She gladly helped herself to another portion, eating it on the porch, uncaring of the overcast sky as the wind gently blew around her while the memories unlocked by the old photographs swept through her like endorphins after sex. Who were the others in the pictures? Where could they have been taken? Slowly, she remembered many. Others, though, could have been one person or another she could no longer identify with certainty, in places that might have been this club or that old restaurant. One released a particularly vivid memory: a winter's night at the hotel when she had been exceptionally 'on' and everything clicked. The room was full; the mood was good and everyone was listening to her and not, as could sometimes happen, engaged in their own conversations in small groups that sometimes made it feel as though she was being deliberately ignored. The room was hers and Henry had shown up unexpectedly and sat listening with an obvious pride in her that she had rarely seen. He even played a few numbers at Paige's request to the delight of everyone there. Afterward, at three in the morning, Paige and Henry, along with a handful of diehard fans, went for a walk in Central Park while the snow fell — a night Paige remembered describing as 'magical.' With a bottle of Champagne and glasses Henry had taken from the Hotel, they skated through the park with a light snow falling, and the several people in tow including her biggest fan: an elderly television news producer who walked with a cane but was carried along by the others, smiling his toothy grin, as if a young child on Christmas morning while everyone raised their glasses and sang holiday songs. How did these snapshots happen? Who could have been responsible? Who had given them to her? Paige hadn't a clue. But the photos of the happy, flash-it faces in the surrounding darkness of Central Park in the middle of the night, uncaring of any potential danger, and with falling snowflakes illuminated like fireflies were indeed a gift. A magical gift.

Her hunger sated, Paige put the dish and utensils in the sink. Returning to the attic, manila envelope in hand, she, for the first time since Henry's death, passed the piano as though it were just another stick of furniture, never thinking that she must try to get back to playing it. The only thing that mattered to her at that moment was the lure of the old trunk and what was still to be discovered within it. Paige hoped to find more photographs as she again sat on the floor beside it. Reaching deep inside under what was piled on the surface, she touched a book made of suede, grabbed onto it and pulled it out. She immediately knew what it was: the book in which, years ago, she had kept notes about her life in the city. It was bound with a suede tie, like a diary. She remembered buying it at a shop in Grand Central one day many years ago while waiting for a train, which was delayed, for the ride back upstate. Back then she wanted to write. Henry had his painting in addition to his music; she had craved another creative outlet. Her plan had been to write a memoir eventually, maybe in novel form. She certainly had enough characters from her nights at the hotel to populate a novel, and liked the idea of couching it all as fiction so only those individuals involved would know what was true and what wasn't. Stiff from the years of the weight placed upon it, the spine crackled as Paige slowly pulled the cover open. She recognized the small, careful handwriting as her own; line upon line of it on the blank, white paper. Notes about her life written exclusively on the train during the commute to and from the city. No visual aids were needed when she wrote them, but now, without her eyeglasses, she could not see more than an undecipherable blur of blue ink. Paige had known she could write well. Henry, who was a tough critic about everything, told her so and had encouraged her. He had wanted her to write her novel. 'Get on with it, Paige!' he used to tell her. "Make me a stinker in it if you want, but get on with it!' Henry often told her to *Get on with it!* Paige liked that about him. He always pushed her to develop her creativity; to turn an idea into reality. The novel, however, never happened, though she always told herself that it still might one day. Now she held the long-lost material for it in her hands.

Paige was impressed with the style her younger self had put to the paper. She read about that elderly former news producer with the impressive past career who sat 'gnome-like and alone, chin on his cane' nearly every night in the Metropolitan, his eyes trained solely upon Paige, often *shhhh*-ing sternly anyone who dared speak too loudly. Paige knew he was enamored of her; he made no secret of it and was undeterred in expressing it, even when Paige would speak to him about Henry. She wrote about how he often insisted on driving her home in his dilapidated old Pontiac, his eyes barely able to see over the steering wheel as he talked non-stop about how he might help her career with the contacts he'd had. There were recollections of the elderly woman regular who claimed to have been a Romanov princess; about sexual advances from several men and more than a few women. Then flipping through more sheets of paper she stumbled upon a craggy box drawn in red pen. Inside it she had written: *I am sure to feel differently on another day, but on the train back to the city I am relieved to leave Henry's orb of neurosis, negativity, criticism and obsession with death.* Paige sat stunned at what was written in her hand. Later entries revealed the same boxed-in script with passages such as: *I see no hope for improvement, only sadness beyond depression and tears; He is making me die too; There is no room for love, laughter, life; I feel depression beyond sadness – beyond tears; I look forward to a life free of him.*

The wooden floor seemed to creak under the weight Paige felt pressing on her. Going numb, she began to shake, feverish with the memories now flooding her mind. This was what life with Henry had been like. Caring for him over the course of the last year had overwhelmed everything else. His death had created a void into which all the memories had vanished. *I don't want to hear another word from him unless it is goodbye!* Paige read. *I feel like I am dying with every breath.* Dropping the notebook on the floor, she struggled to her feet and quickly left the attic, needing to steady herself by holding the railing on the way down the staircase. In the living room she collapsed onto the sofa. Still trembling, she recalled the day, years before, when she arrived home from the city to find Henry screwing one of his music students on the floor by the piano, not six feet from where she now sat. That unexpected sight had sent her gasping for breath and back to the train station. Out of the house. This house. Her house. The house she now inhabited alone. Though she had not seen the entry in the notebook, she could suddenly vividly remember what she had written with a trembling hand: *I wish he would just die!!!* Back in the city apartment, Paige lay in bed, two bottles of wine drunk, waiting for a phone call from Henry. She waited for his apologizing, making excuses, assigning blame — yet the call never came. They were fornicating on the small carpet by the piano. Their carpet. The one they had purchased together. Paige recalled the way she and Henry had made love on it several times when they were still passionate about each other. Nothing was sacred to Henry. Everything was his and his alone; to do with whatever the hell he pleased.

The thought that they might not have even noticed her walk in on them, putting the onus on Paige to deal with it; either in a confrontation or by burying it deep inside herself. Could she have been to blame? Their lovemaking had become routine. For years Paige had not had any real interest in it, submitting passively to Henry, always hoping it would be quick and not too tiresome. The realization that Henry had always put her in that situation: the position of being the one to deal with it. Always, he managed to escape responsibility. Confronting him, Paige knew, would result in such a burst of rage that she would shut down immediately. Swallowing it would stifle her will to live. That was the reality of much of her forty-year-long life with Henry. Recognizing that reality was discordant and therefore horrible; an absolute betrayal of the very concept of love. She regretted everything; their life together; the way she had cared for him while he was so sick; running herself ragged to support the two of them, even when he was well and able, he sat home doing nothing except feeling sorry for himself, sometimes threatening suicide. So often he made Paige feel small with cruel criticism of her ability as a pianist; criticism she knew was unwarranted but was hurtful, nevertheless. And wasn't that the whole point? Wasn't that the whole and entire point? Just to hurt and to injure; to make her feel inferior because he knew so well that she wasn't? Paige knew there was much more venom in that notebook and in others she had written over the years. The old trunk now seemed filled with it. It wasn't necessary that she read them all; recollections now overwhelmed her consciousness.

Why can't I remember? Whether the name of the damned jazz club where I first saw Henry play was *Fusion* or *Fission*? It was something she had always known and thought she could never forget. It didn't matter; either way it was correct. The club had been the place she discovered her irresistible attraction to Henry, even as it had split her emotionally from George. Still, Paige found the fact that she could not remember something so fundamental disturbing. Age, she feared, had begun to ravage her mind. Should it continue until the last forty years had been entirely erased, she might be happier; she might be able to begin anew. A life without regret or anger. Out of nowhere, the recollection of one night at the club when, during a break, there was a sudden loud altercation at the bar involving Max Schulze, a bass player from Hamburg who sometimes jammed with Henry. The club manager warned Henry that Max's infamous temper would not be tolerated in the club again. Henry defended his friend, whose talents he genuinely admired, saying the fight couldn't have been Max's doing because no self-respecting German would ever start an argument unless it would result in at least fifty-million casualties, and there were never more than fifty people in the club at any one time. 'Besides, he's got a heart as sweet as Oma's last piece of marzipan, don't you Max?' Henry said, pinching Max's cheek. He could defuse any tense situation with wry humor when he cared to.

Sitting on the sofa in the living room of the house, alone now without Henry, with the daily imperative of earning a living on hold and unable to distract her, Paige felt as though she had emerged from the fog of her mourning and could now clearly see the past that had been buried by the endless trivialities of daily life. She had pursued him. It was because of her that Henry divorced his wife. That was stamped in her mind. It always had been. She was responsible. Her actions, the choices she had made, had resulted in unhappiness for Henry's wife and was responsible for the life she herself had lived. Paige had carried animus for Henry within her for a very long time. Even when he was so ill, there were times when Paige could not help displaying the subconscious arrogance the healthy sometimes have over the sick; though maybe in her case it wasn't subconscious. Maybe she had been deliberately mean, punishing him for the choices she had made. The old trunk pulled Paige back to it as if by a magnetic force. She was suddenly consumed with the strange sensation of wanting to know what caused her to lead the life she had lived, and why, exactly, she harbored such hostility toward Henry. Maybe then she could find a clue about Henry's animosity toward her. Thinking of the past, it was clear that he obviously did resent her. The trunk with its magical powers of shifting time might hold a clue. Back upstairs, Paige again sat on the floor next to it and began carefully removing its tightly-packed contents, one thing at a time, and placing them neatly on the floor by her side. There was everything imaginable: envelopes stuffed with old receipts and tax declarations; a heavy brass candlestick she long ago thought had been lost; more of her notebooks, which she set to one side; many old books of sheet music; then a crushed shoe box, its lid broken and seams split apart at two corners. It contained small, spiral-bound appointment books that had belonged to Henry; books going back decades, which Paige had never before seen. Strangely for a jazz musician, Henry had been organized and fastidious about everything when they met; a characteristic that had waned later in life as he got older and grumpier. Paige flipped through each of the appointment books to see that they were filled with Henry's handwriting as she organized them according to the years, put them back into the shoe box, and carried them downstairs to the living room. Sitting on the sofa with the box on her lap she felt a sharp tingling of anxiety rippling through her; a combination of anticipation and apprehension. Had Henry kept these from her on purpose? Or were they so mundane that it would never have occurred to him to share them with her? But if that were the case, why keep them all these years? Then again, Henry was one of those people who never threw anything away willingly. He probably found them in the back of a closet and decided to just put them in the trunk with the old tax returns and other things that one simply wanted out of the way but not thrown away. Nevertheless, here were details from his life, as close as he would ever come to writing a diary. Henry was not a writer like Paige and had no aspirations to ever become one. Yet he did at one time have aspirations to become great; a known musician equal to his talents as he saw them. What he felt was his destiny had eluded him, which was the reason, Paige always thought, that he could often be so bitter and angry in his later years. The earliest appointment book was from 1979 and contained only the most ordinary of appointment reminders; nothing of any consequence as far as Paige was concerned. Neither did 1980. It was not until 1981 that Henry had written anything close to a recollection. A simple 'P' followed by an exclamation point on a day he noted that he was playing at a club cited only by its address in Chicago. Paige knew the 'P' meant her. She struggled with the date; how far into their relationship could it have been? Not very far. Henry had probably written only a 'P' to hide her existence from his wife. Or was Paige reading something into this one letter of the alphabet that bore no relationship to reality? Filled with a sense of nervous queasiness she tried to make sense of it. In a moment, that vague uneasiness crystalized into an urgent need. She had to discover what she had really meant to Henry; something that had been eating away inside her since his death. Goddamn it, Henry, why did you have to be so cryptic about every fucking thing? That 'P' must stand for me! She flipped through the appointment books of each succeeding year, noticing that 'P' entered from time to time among random notes and appointments. Eventually, they did give way to the name

'Paige' right around the time she remembered Henry had moved out of the apartment he had shared with his wife. I was right! He was thinking about me. Even when he feigned boredom at my very existence, he thought enough of me to mark the date he had seen me at the club in his appointment books! Like a schoolboy with a crush! How sweet! Why couldn't you ever tell me this, Henry? Why are you making me scrounge over every inch of this house after you're dead to try and find clues about your feelings for me? And again, the resentment returned. That is what Henry had reduced her to after four decades together. On the verge of tears, she sat there, unsure whether she was mourning Henry's loss, or the fact that she had stayed with him so long.

How unnecessary it all was, the pain she was now experiencing, being alone in the house and wondering what she had meant to the man she had spent practically her entire life with. It could have been so much less painful if he had simply told her how he felt; if he had just abandoned his dumb 'I'm a deep-thinking artist' charade. They had no interest in formally marrying; it was so. . .

establishment. But why couldn't he have brought it up just once? Just to let me know I meant something? Why couldn't he, just once in his life, have made himself as vulnerable as everyone else is? Why couldn't he have done so just with me? Paige recalled the only time she had formally met Henry's wife, Ruth; at her surprise when Ruth called and suggested they meet at a café in Chicago. It seemed so strange that, at first, she was frightened by the prospect. But Henry had no family beyond the aunt who raised him, whom he always referred to as "Aunt Tits" because of her enormous bosom. Paige was intensely curious about the kind of woman Henry had chosen to become his family. She knew her only from Henry's point of view, which was that Ruth was a bland and colorless personality with whom he felt as though he were living in purgatory. Paige was surprised by how different she was from what she had imagined. Ruth was a very attractive and intelligent woman of Henry's age, and although Paige had agreed to meet her only because she was curious about what kind of woman Henry had married, she still vividly remembered suffering a good deal of last-minute anxiety before the meeting, which

Henry knew nothing about. But she forged ahead with the reasoning that she would be taking Ruth's place in Henry's life, and so she wanted to know more about her; that in knowing Ruth, she might be able to learn more about Henry. Paige could recall only one thing Ruth had said verbatim: 'You are a very beautiful, young woman. You can have anyone. And you are choosing an empty shell of a man. Be prepared to carry him for the rest of your life.' At that moment, Paige was struck, not as much by what Ruth had said—she was prepared to hear negative feelings for obvious reasons—but that she said it all so blandly, without the slightest trace of bitterness or malice. Yet Paige, so desperately in love with Henry, felt that Ruth must have been calculating in wanting to meet in the first place, hiding her bitterness by talking in a way that showed she didn't give a damn about either of them. Paige now, sitting alone in the house, regretted not talking more to Ruth; not asking more about Henry. She had the awful feeling that Ruth probably knew Henry better after twelve years of marriage than she did after spending forty years of her life with him.

Paige could not help wondering what became of Ruth, and whether she had gone on to have a more fulfilling life after Henry than she herself had had with him. At least Ruth knew what she had meant to Henry, if only because he had divorced her. If Ruth was still alive, Henry was now consigned to a small corner of her life as a flawed personality and a failed relationship. It was a long ago closed case; one that could not be regarded as more than a dumb but minor mistake at this point in her life. Paige could not decide whether to envy or hate her for that. There had to have been a time when Ruth had been as attracted to Henry as she had been. Yet Ruth was able to abandon him without looking back. Perhaps, Paige thought, that was because they didn't have the same kind of deep connection that she and Henry shared. Ruth was not a musician. Her family had money, and she was a patron of the arts, but she was not an artist of any kind herself. Ruth did not *create* the way Paige and Henry did. She was not capable of it, having neither the inclination nor the talent. Paige wondered why they had been attracted to each other at all. Ruth was certainly physically attractive, but Henry had to have met plenty of women just as pretty. Could Henry have married Ruth only for her money and connections? Could he have been that cold and conniving? Paige knew that there were not many people as enamored of Henry as she was. Not in the beginning. Paige had always thought she had seen something in him that others could not; that she understood Henry in ways others were never able to. It was the reason she tolerated his moods and bad behavior, especially in his later years. Now she wasn't so sure. Maybe all these years she had been fooling herself simply because she could never admit having been so wrong about him. Simple human nature would have dictated that the more time she had invested in him, the harder it would have been to acknowledge the truth and leave him. Maybe the world had seen Henry the way Ruth evidently had: as momentarily interesting and amusing, then as a bore as time wore on. But Paige had never found Henry boring. Tedious sometimes, but never boring. When she was young, she had dreaded both tedium and boredom. Even by young adolescence, Paige had already considered her parents' relationship tedious and boring. She had told herself that the kind of ordinary, middle-class life they led was something she would avoid. And, aware of her beauty from a very young age, Paige was always certain she would have her pick of men who would show her another kind of life. She had chosen Henry over George. Yet she had to pursue Henry. George, like all the others, had always chased her. Paige had always known that to be one of the reasons she found Henry so different. As with many things in life, nothing that comes easy is worth having. Yet she thought of where their relationship had left her: grieving alone on the sofa in an empty house with a telephone that had stopped ringing. She now felt a good measure of guilt and shame at the way she had internalized her negative views about her parents' marriage. She remembered, when she was very young, her father coming home from work, entering the house shouting, 'Where are my girls?!' The natural happiness in his voice; as though it had been the one thing he had been looking forward to all day. How nice that must have been for him. How nice it must have been for her mother to hear. Paige never forgot the feeling of security and love she instinctively felt when she heard it as a young girl. While it was her mother who had always encouraged her piano playing, to the extent that she needed encouragement, it was her father who reveled in happiness, heaping his praise on her when she played for him. And it was he who had the idea of surprising Paige with a piano. 'It was your father's idea,' she remembered her mother telling her once. "I don't know what made him think you would enjoy it, but he did.' She recalled that afternoon—two days after she had turned sixteen years old, coming home from school, not to find her mother, as usual doing housework or starting to prepare dinner, but her Aunt Sally, cat-eye glasses and bouffant hairdo, distressed and alone in the house, her voice loud and shaken when she said, *Oh Paige, something terrible has happened!* Paige had often thought back on that moment: how a day that started like any other, with her father leaving the house after breakfast as he always did, had, within just a few hours, caused life to go haywire. It was the moment she learned that her father had suffered a heart attack at work and had been sent to the hospital; the moment, for the very first time in her life, that Paige had experienced real, bone-chilling fear. She could still recall the shock she felt at her first sight of her once vibrant father, lying in his hospital bed, unshaven, not quite aware of what was going on around him. It was two months before he would be in his home again, a shadow of his former self; a severely debilitated stranger now living in the house. A surge of nausea as she clearly recalled once thinking to herself, *Why does he have to be here?* 'Fear, numbness, callousness,' Paige mumbled; a stream of consciousness running through her mind, as though an epiphany had laid out a roadmap of her emotional development. Early in her life she had become desensitized to the world; only the piano seemed to connect her with reality. Her father had grown angry over his condition as the years passed; bitter over his life unjustly taken. Often he would vent his frustrations on her mother, who was the sole person by his side. Neighbors and friends drifted away after their initial show of concern and support. Paige's mother had to work in order to support the family at a time when most other women her age were stay-at-home moms. Her father died many years later, when Paige was thirty-five years old. She had been quietly shocked at the depth of her mother's wrenching grief, even though his condition had meant a life of hardship for her; hardship that had only increased with age. Could that have been the real reason I stayed with Henry? Because he was impossible to become too close to? So I would never suffer the way my mother did after my father died? But now I am suffering precisely because Henry had never opened himself up to me; never let me know what, if anything, I had really meant to him. If I was the one who was now gone, he would surely continue as he had always done, with not much hurt. Maybe he would miss me from time to time, but Henry was always so obviously content to be alone in his later years. And I'm sure there were other things in his life he no longer had, or was able to do, that he missed from time to time. He adapted; just learned to go on without them. I would be just one more of those things. That thought hurt Paige as painfully as a knife to the gut. It had her obsessing over what the letter 'P' written decades ago by Henry in a book of unimportant appointments could possibly mean. The pain Paige had been feeling turned to humiliation at that thought. Henry had a knack for humiliating her while he was alive. Now he was doing it from the grave.

For the first time in a great many years, Paige experienced an intense longing for her parents and the innocence of her childhood. The forty-years-long emotional roller coaster with Henry had so greedily hoarded her life that there didn't seem time to dwell on much else. Overcome by an aching nostalgia, she went to the piano and sat down before the keyboard, trying to remember the songs she played for her father that he loved so much so long ago. Yet, still, she was unable to force more than a single note, finding the sound she had made—sounds that were once the very essence of her being—grating to her very core. Paige stood up from the piano with the feeling that, this too, Henry had taken from her. She went upstairs to the bedroom, where, in a bottom dresser drawer, she took out an old, leather-bound album filled with photos from her childhood, which, for reasons that eluded her, she had not looked in many, many years. She wanted to be with her parents again; to a time before Henry, and the move to the city, and this house. Seeing her father, mother and herself, all still young, elbowed Henry from Paige's mind. Her fingers moved gently over the old black-and-white photographs, as if she were reading the emotions she was feeling in braille. Her heart ached at the same time she felt joy; emotions which manifested themselves as tears welling up in her eyes. She saw her mother and father together in the years before he had become ill; the family's tail-finned car; the three of them together at a family gathering, which included her maternal grandfather, whom she barely remembered but had always known as gentle and kind. Other photos included a trip to a park; a zoo; on a road trip; and of course, photos, many photos of her at a piano. She felt a surge of sorrow and guilt; as if she had forsaken them all for Henry. Yet the feelings for her parents and childhood had caused any thought of Henry to evaporate. As if he ceased to exist, not by death, but through the simple tedium of thinking so much about him.

Paige took the album and the heavy candlestick, which she had always liked, and went downstairs. She put the candlestick on a bookshelf, went to the kitchen and boiled some water for tea. She was also feeling hungry and cut herself a piece of almost stale pound cake. With the tea prepared, she had intended to go onto the back porch, but it had gotten windy, cold, and had turned menacingly darker outside. Sitting at the kitchen table, she turned the album's stiff pages. Later photos of Paige with her father in his debilitated, crippled state, his face passing for what was a smile, and the three of them together, smiling, as though all was perfectly normal and right with the world. Paige had never forgotten feelings of abandonment as her mother turned all her attention toward her father. The exact instant her father's heart seized in his chest was the moment any remnant of Paige's childhood ended. Later she would feel intense guilt over the enmity she had felt toward her father for taking her mother away from her; for making sure that no matter how hard Paige tried, she would never again experience the same doting love from her. She recalled sitting at the piano for hours after coming home from school rather than interacting with her father while waiting for her mother to return from work. Throughout her young life, Paige had enjoyed being an only child, and could never understand why people had always asked if she would like a younger brother or sister to play with. But the days after school, after everything had changed, she had wished there had been siblings to relieve the burden of her father from her. There were school friends; names and young faces she could still remember: Dark-haired Anna, Redheaded Maura, Loraine with the kinky-blonde head. But she rarely was able to see them outside school. She needed to stay with her father, to relieve the home health aide they could barely afford, until her mother returned. And she would never invite those friends to her home. Not with her father confined to the house the way he was. Paige was embarrassed by him. The piano had become a refuge for her as she pushed herself to learn ever more complex pieces in the hope of again getting the love and attention she had once received from her mother, but would never again experience up to the day of her mother's death. Paige remembered playing more loudly when her father called for her in a sound that came to pass for her name. Her father's words were often incomprehensible noises by then, which only her mother seemed able to decipher.

Paige now admitted to herself that, in her callous resentment toward him, she simply didn't care to hear his words. She was overcome by awful guilt; the guilt of wondering what her terrible avoidance of her father could have done to him emotionally; whether the change in his little girl's behavior toward him became too much to bear, hindering any possible semblance of recovery, and whether it might have contributed to his deteriorating condition. 'I'm so sorry, daddy,' she said out loud as her head fell into her hands and the tears that flooded her eyes dropped onto her lap. She sobbed uncontrollably, 'Please forgive me. I was too young and selfish. I know you didn't want to get sick. Please, please forgive me, daddy. I love you so much!'

It took some time before Paige was able to overcome her emotion. As she did she could not help wondering again if her mother was the reason she had rejected George in favor of Henry; the man she could never hope to get close to. And not just George. There had been other relationships with men before him; relationships in which Paige had manufactured or magnified slight flaws of character in order to convince herself that none of them would be capable of giving her happiness.

How rotten she had been to them; to start one relationship after another, relationships in which she gave herself fully before abruptly removing herself from their lives. Paige knew that she had hurt those men every bit as much as she had hurt George, and realized now that on some level she had enjoyed doing so. That in making them feel inadequate, or in some way broken, she had been forcing them to feel what she had found so painful in the inattention her mother had shown her after her father had fallen ill. Paige remembered a voice she could no longer attach to a face telling her that one day she would wake up completely alone. She realized that today was that day; that in reality she had been the broken one. How cruel fate had been to her family. How wonderful their lives could have been if her father had never suffered his heart attack; if she had been able to feel the simple satisfaction of a man who had loved her for who she was instead of, for reasons now inexplicable, feeling the impulsive need to find fault where there was none; to intentionally destroy what might have turned out to be perfectly good.

There was a large envelope between the last page and the back cover of the photo album. It contained yet more photographs; pictures Paige had found at her mother's house while she was clearing it out after her death. There was also an old handwritten note from her mother telling Paige that Henry had written her 'the most beautiful and touching' letter of condolence after her father died. Paige couldn't remember ever seeing the letter. She had never even known Henry had written it. He had never told her of it. Paige thought Henry incapable of doing something so kind. Yet he had, and without saying a word to her about it. Unlike herself, Henry had always treated Paige's parents with respect. He was always very kind to her father, carrying on patient conversations with him as though unknowing of his disability. Henry always seemed to have a calming influence on her father, who, since his illness, was often quick to become agitated and angry. Henry always seemed to genuinely like and care about

Paige's parents. Henry, who could be so scornful and critical of and withdrawn with everyone else, was always helpful and considerate toward them. He would take her father by the elbow and gently help him walk while conversing with him. When Henry did that, Paige thought that her father could almost feel normal again. The only reason Paige could imagine for Henry's behavior was that they were her parents. They were important to him because they were hers. And was that not a way of showing his love for her? She recalled how, weeks after her father's funeral, she experienced a moment when she fell apart, ridden with guilt for the feeling of having abandoned him by moving to New York, and how Henry held her and movingly said that her father harbored no such feelings of abandonment; that he had always been proud of his daughter and that he loved her very much. He knew this, he said, because her father had told him many times during the walks they had taken together. Perhaps her grief, her bitterness at being left alone, had caused her to resent Henry. And how unfair and selfish that was. He, after all, was the one who had suffered and died. He was the one who could no longer experience a sunrise, or sit on the back porch with the cool wind running through the trees.

Her ill-will toward Henry caused feelings of shame in Paige. He wasn't an unyieldingly hard man devoid of emotions. She recalled how he cried inconsolably when he was told that Aunt Tits had died unexpectedly, and how stunned she was by it. There was a time when she had thought Henry was cruelly taunting his aunt with that name. Not until she finally met Aunt Tits did it became clear that the woman actually enjoyed being referred to that way; that everyone in the neighborhood called her "Tits." It was all so wonderfully good-natured. For Henry, calling her by that name was an act of love. Growing up, he was not in the least embarrassed or disturbed at the idea of being raised by a single woman the world referred to as "Tits." In fact, he reveled in the humor of it all; so eternally grateful was he to her for taking him in as a twelve-year-old boy. In time, Paige found it impossible to even consider calling Henry's aunt anything else; she did have the biggest pair of tits Paige had ever seen. The memory of it all produced a short burst of a laugh that was more like a sneeze; her first feeling of lightness since Henry had died and for weeks prior to his death. A moment in which the denseness of her bereavement was lifted. Yet how quickly it turned to pity. Poor Henry. Imagine losing both your parents the way he did, and at such an early age; to be so young and so alone in the world. He was also an only child. Music was his refuge, too. Longing to feel close to him, Paige moved to the piano. Again she lifted the fallboard and touched the keys lightly without pressing on them. Any sound she produced without Henry there to hear it would merely be another betrayal of him. Paige covered the keys yet again. Yet her need to be close to Henry was so strong that she felt compelled to go to the bedroom. Sitting at the foot of the bed on which she had slept alone night after night since Henry's death in no way brought the emotional relief Paige needed to end the sharp ache of loss tingling in her chest and radiating through her limbs. A rush of desperate energy tinged with a vague sense of hope pushed her up the stairs to the attic. Unconcerned with the reasons she had been avoiding it, Paige threw open the door to

Henry's art studio, as if in anticipation of finding him there. The stark emptiness that permeated the studio since Henry died had not abated. She entered slowly, almost cautiously, as if trying to avoid adding yet another emotional injury to those she was already enduring, and sat down in the chair in front of Henry's easel. His nearly completed landscape painting featuring a slender young woman in a yellow sundress on her knees beside a lake had to be abandoned more than a year ago; his physical state had made it impossible for him to tolerate anything but a recumbent positon for long periods. Paige surveyed the brushes in small glass jars of turpentine; the old, wooden mahl stick that Henry had owned since they met; the palette knives and wooden palette stained with swipes of dried color—all still exactly where he had set them down, as if waiting in vain hope of the artist's return.

Paige sat in the chair before Henry's unfinished work, examining the brush strokes made by his hand; the way the woman's loose-fitting dress followed the contours of her shape as she knelt on both knees gazing out at the lake. Gradually, the aching and slightly prickly sensation of loss she had been experiencing throughout her being began to consolidate in her chest, producing a trembling in her limbs and shortness of breath that Paige could not control. Struggling to stand, her hand on the back of the chair slipped with the weight she had been putting on it, knocking the chair onto its side. Paige stumbled out of the studio and down the stairs to the bedroom where she fell onto the bed, hyperventilating, unable to catch her breath. Only by sitting up was she able to eventually regain her composure and her breathing, just as she was contemplating dialing *911*.

'Henry, Henry, Henry,' she murmured in a weary voice, sitting on the side of the bed and looking at the floor. Too restless to lie down, or to stay in that room, she made her way, exhausted, downstairs. After pouring herself a glass of water from the kitchen sink she went to the living room and sat on the sofa. A few moments later, giving in to fatigue, Paige laid herself down on it with one arm across her face. She wanted to sleep, but her mind, though fatigued, was too active, too driven to think about her life both before and after

Henry. Restless and disturbed by the fact that there were still so many questions, that she felt so unfulfilled after so much of their lives had been spent together, Paige could not stop wondering what it was about him that she had found so fascinating all those years ago. Naturally, people change over decades as their lives shrink, and time grows ever shorter; with options becoming fewer and further between until there are eventually none left. Yet life keeps going, regardless of the needs that would never now be satisfied. What was it about him when she was young, with so much life still to be lived, and so many options available to her, that caused Paige to fall so desperately in love with him? Again she remembered how arrogant he was the first few times she had met him, and how much she disliked that about him. Of course, she had been impressed with his musicality, but she had been at least as impressed by other musicians she had met back then and since. She didn't fall in love with any of them, despite the fact that many were attractive and charming personalities. Nor had Paige ever been intimidated by any of the men she had one relationship after another with. She had been easily able to wrap them around her finger, to bend them to her will, just as she had done with George. She tried thinking clinically: What chemical reaction in her brain did Henry trigger that caused her to need him so much? So much so that everything was subjugated to him? Paige recalled how intimidated she was by Henry in the beginning. That she had to push herself to talk to him during his breaks at the club. She could see in her mind's eye, even decades later, how sheepishly she had approached him. She could still hear her vacillating and nervous voice. There were times she actually stammered, noticing Henry's slight grin as she did so, as though he had enjoyed inspiring that kind of awe in someone. She berated herself in her mind when that happened, feeling so foolish that she wanted to go away and never come back. No other man had ever managed to make Paige feel so insecure. She had been in control of every relationship she had ever been in, right up until she decided to end them. Yet the allure of Henry was too great to let her humiliation cause her to disappear, no matter how much she may have wanted to. A week or ten days would pass before Paige would return to the club to see him, with or without George, as though enough time had passed that the slate of embarrassment was wiped clean and forgotten.

The exhaustion in Paige won out as she fell into an uneasy sleep on the sofa. Yet, even in sleep, her overwrought mind worked; even as she fell more deeply into desperately wanted rest, the sudden sensation of freefalling coinciding with the senseless thought that Henry and Ruth were together again without her startled Paige back into full, and wide-awake consciousness with her heart racing.

She sat up on the sofa with hollow emptiness radiating from the center of her chest outward through her limbs; that sensation she had felt so often since Henry's death. It had a vague familiarity, close to what she felt as a young girl when her father had fallen ill; a longing for the life that was no more. A longing that submerged with time, but had always remained somewhere inside her and was as recognizable to this day as it was when she was young. Simultaneously, for the first time, she knew that penetratingly desolate feeling as yet something else. It was the sensation she would experience when she was young and needed to move on from a relationship; the feeling that anything other than her music would eventually become empty and unhinged from her. The time when some new stimulation was needed to make her feel attached to the world around her again. It was the lack of feeling that fed her compulsive cold-heartedness. Were it only so easy to rid the current, painful emptiness with a young flirt, even temporarily, as it was back then, she thought.

Seeking to distract her agitated mind, Paige again turned on the TV. She sat with the remote in her outstretched hand, robotically moving from one channel to another; one at a time, number after number, more than one hundred of them, stopping only momentarily at something that might have caught her attention when things were normal, but now seemed irrelevant, mindless and intrusive. Defeated, she switched off the TV and her limp arm fell onto the sofa cushion with the remote still in her hand.

Her thoughts wandered to the early days in the club; of the times when Ruth was also there. Paige would approach Henry after he had finished for the evening, carefully calculating what to tell him of the intricacies of this or that number, always in the hope that Henry would invite her to sit at the piano and play. Ruth would suddenly appear out of nowhere and say something about getting the car, or being tired and wanting to get home; mundane statements that would land like a crashing ten-ton safe, ruining it all. When that happened it left Paige feeling like a young and stupid groupie. Sometimes she thought Ruth did it intentionally as a show of possession and control; a way of marking her territory. Henry had thrown Paige's self-confidence so off kilter that it did not even occur to her then that Ruth perceived her as a threat. Thinking about it now, so many years later, was like pondering an episode of *Wild Kingdom* that dealt with the mating habits of apes or penguins. For Paige, Ruth was a displeasing woman. She showed no real interest in Henry as a musician. She would occasionally attend his gigs, sitting at a table as though he needed her there for emotional support. Sometimes

Ruth would talk loudly to others during his sets, which to any musician was sacrilegious. She could not understand why Henry would marry a woman like that. Contemplating that question at the time sometimes made Paige wonder why she should even bother interacting with him. But always hidden in her memory was the brief scene she had witnessed near the entrance to the coat check, when Ruth grabbed Henry's forearm in anger while shouting, then lowering her voice, and Henry pulling it away with a pained expression on his face before disappearing into the coat-check room. Paige was saddened by that, and the thought of it, even decades later, could inspire feelings of pity for Henry in her. Paige thought then how easy her relationship with George was. She likened it to the one her parents had before her father fell ill. Henry, for all his talent, had been made to seem small by Ruth, like a young child, scolded, and in a venue that he felt he ruled; a place where people paid money to see him. For a time after witnessing that, Paige had felt the base instincts of motherhood aroused in her, and had wanted to go into the cloakroom and console him. Yet fearing embarrassment, either for Henry or for herself, she did not. When George appeared behind her, asking if she was ready to go, Paige turned her back and went home with him as usual.

Standing at the door to the porch, she looked out over the yard. It was still overcast and windy; the cool air brushing her skin through the leaky doorframe was not unpleasant. Paige had always enjoyed standing there at certain times of the year, feeling the cold air outside the house lightly touching her while it was warm within. She recounted the various ways the view had changed since they had moved here: aside from the saplings that were now towering trees, the 'farm', a good-sized dirt patch that had once been the vegetable garden she had tended to over a great many summers, was gone, now displaced by various types of wild grasses, small vines and weeds. She imagined the portion of it that Henry had taken over for the marijuana plants he tenderly cultivated for years, long after Paige had given up vegetable gardening, until he was no longer able. Shoots of memories began pushing up through decades of life. There were many hilarious stories attached to Henry's marijuana garden. Dreamy and contemplative, Paige pictured the day she had returned from the supermarket, putting the brown paper bags on the kitchen counter and noticing Henry showing Charlotte and her fifteen-year-old son, Eddie, the vegetable garden. She joined them when Charlotte pointed to Henry's marijuana plants, 'And what are these odd looking things?' 'Uh . . . those are Japanese maples. I dry the leaves and put them in ice tea.' 'Oh, isn't that interesting.' The next morning all of Henry's marijuana plants had been stripped of their leaves. 'It was that little fucker, Eddie! He stole my weed! He knew what he was lookin' at; I saw it in his eyes. I'm going over there and getting it back!' 'And what are you going to tell his mother? You're gonna accuse Eddie of stealing your Japanese maple plants? Why on earth would he bother?' 'I'll just tell her what it really is. Why not get the little rat in some hot water while I'm at it?' 'You know his father is a detective, right?' 'Who's a detective?' 'Charlotte's husband. Jerry is a detective.' 'Goddamn it! What is it with kids these days?' Paige had many affectionate memories of evenings getting high over a bottle of wine at the piano with Henry; a ritual that came with the house and had been buried with his death.

Paige went upstairs to the bedroom and, from a dresser drawer, pulled out Henry's 'stash'; a plastic sandwich bag with a couple of ounces of his marijuana and pipe. Paige had last used it during the end stages of his illness, to relieve his pain and reduce her own stress. Downstairs in the kitchen she filled the small pipe and lit it, inhaling deeply. She soon felt buzzed and regretted not having done it sooner and more often over the last few weeks. The reserve of three letter-sized envelopes of Henry's dried cannabis may have become somewhat stale, but they seemed neither ownerless nor orphaned. They were a gift; an offering extended by Henry's quirky spirit. Paige felt herself smiling. Japanese maple plants. Henry was always quick on his feet that way; always good at coming up with something plausible. Henry's lies always seemed plausible. A memory from out of nowhere: Henry not yet debilitated, but in a foul mood, lying in a hospital bed, being visited by a nurse who told him that music students from the nearby high school sometimes came to play for patients as a way to cheer them up. 'Oh, just kill me now,' Henry told the nurse, rubbing his fatigued face. Thoughts of sitting at the piano and attempting to play crossed her mind but were soon abandoned; not by a lack of will this time, but pushed aside by the vague notion that it was still 'too soon.'

Standing again at the door to the porch, the pleasant sensation of the cool draft on her skin was heightened by the marijuana. The memory shoots began pushing more easily through the earthen-caked years of past events. Paige went to the sink, filled the teapot with water and put it on the stove, recalling the night at the club when Henry finally did seem interested or maybe amused enough to ask, offhandedly, if Paige would play something. She took a seat at the piano as Henry gathered sheet music and the room, empty of patrons, was being cleaned up. Paige played her own composition; a melodious, rolling celebration of autumn that she had been working on for several months. With her fingers moving effortlessly from one end of the keyboard to the other she could see Henry, who was leaning down, stuffing his leather satchel suddenly freeze, as though captivated by the notes Paige was producing; as if experiencing something he had never expected. Paige easily recalled Henry's expression as he stood up and listened with arms crossed, chin in his hand, obviously taking pleasure at the sounds she made. She remembered the satisfaction she felt as her fingers danced effortlessly over the keys, knowing fully her ability and taking pride in it. The few employees who were left in the club had stopped what they were doing and applauded. Henry smiled, told her she was wonderful, wanting to know about the composition, 'Is that yours?' then immediately offered his thoughts about changing the color of some of the notes by shifting the weight of her hands at certain points; not with the arrogance Paige had been used to from him, but as a fellow musician of ability, just wanting to experiment a bit to see how it would sound. And it did sound better; livelier and with more depth. That was the moment Henry took Paige seriously. From that night onward he respected her. Did he regard her as an absolute equal? Probably not. He was older and had proven he possessed knowledge that she, despite her raw talent and education, didn't quite yet have. Henry held himself in the highest regard, always. Paige attributed that to his eccentric, artistic soul. She recalled, vividly, Henry's eyes on her, for the first time, in that way she knew well: as if he had now, finally, recognized how attractive she was. She poured hot water from the teapot into her cup, over the already used teabag still within, calmed by the effects of the cannabis, and recalling that moment at the club as the moment her fascination with Henry had morphed into something akin to need. Not just of his approval as an artist, but something more. She had established herself in Henry's eyes. He had praised her talent and he had noticed her physically. Paige could again, decades later, feel the palpable sensation of vanity Henry's recognition produced in her young self as his eyes darted over her body. Something only youth and inexperience could have gotten such gratification from. From then on, Paige would no longer approach Henry like a groupie, but as a confident equal. And as she sat with her hands wrapped around a warm mug of tea in the kitchen of the house that she and Henry had shared for decades, she thought the young, beautiful and talented Paige a very foolish girl.

It was with a certain uneasiness that she recalled the pleasure she got so long ago by assuming that Henry and Ruth, given their relationship, were probably not sleeping together. It was difficult even to imagine them sharing a bed, so contemptuous did they sometimes seem of each other. Paige recalled how she often tried to imagine their relationship of mutual contempt, and how the thought of Henry and Ruth's tumultuous marriage thrilled her. It was the antithesis, not only of the kind of relationship her parents had before her father's heart attack, but of the life she could expect with George, who was so willing to do everything he could to please her. The roiling emotions would be expected from a creative, artistic soul; they had to produce a violent passion, a thought which Paige found stimulating. Much more so than when George once told her that she would 'make an excellent wife.' She had realized for some time that George had bored her. But that was the moment she realized just how stifling she found his company, and how emotionally detached she had become from him. That feeling of intense detachment, of remoteness to the world grew more intense, at first with each passing day, then with every passing hour. As it inevitably would, not only relating to George, but as long as she was in a relationship with him, to everything around her; everything except her music. George could not connect with her musicality. No matter how much he enjoyed listening to music and talking about various musicians, he was not one himself. But Henry was. George would never understand what truly moved her. Henry could.

The mug of tea was empty and cold in her hands as Paige recognized and disdained the emotional dependency Henry had brought out in her when she was young. How she thought of him constantly after the attention he had given her the night she first played for him. Paige thought of Ruth, too. Of the way she used to imagine her engaging in sex with Henry; of the passion and romantic moments they must have once shared at some point in their relationship. Something she never had experienced herself with the men she always found fault with. It was impossible for her to be indifferent to it. Paige needed to possess Henry in order to be in control again; in order to feel connected to reality. She would go to the club as often as possible when Henry was playing, sometimes with George but preferably alone. She noticed how Henry would glance at her and grin when she entered; how he would smile at her during his breaks before he disappeared into the coat check room with a book, as if challenging Paige to follow, which she then did when Ruth was not there. Even when George was with her, Paige would disappear, saying she was off to the ladies' room. She would detour to the coat check, where she and Henry would have intense discussions about music for fifteen minutes or so before he would go back to play another set.

Paige was standing perhaps too close to Henry at the back of the long, narrow room, behind the rack of coats, with the odor of wool still damp from the rain, when he asked if she would like to go to his apartment after the show. It was about two o'clock in the morning.

Paige knew that if Henry was inviting her to his home, Ruth would not be there. But she accepted, knowing it was imprudent and dangerous, precisely because it was so. Because in being reckless, she was able to feel a relationship to the world again. Exactly the opposite of what she felt when together with George.

She recalled with increasing discomfort the sense of satisfaction she felt upon entering their apartment; how large it seemed to her; looking at the various photos of Ruth and Henry, including a wedding photo. Henry bringing glasses of wine from the kitchen, and kissing her after each had taken just one sip. There was no talk of music; not even an observation about the grand piano in the living room. There was no foreplay or romance of any kind. She remembered only submitting to him there on the floor of the living room on some sort of fleecy, white throw rug. Paige wondered how could she have been so callous in sleeping with a married man. And that when she was engaged to George, who, at that moment, she had turned into the clueless fiancé; the fool who was blissfully unaware that the woman he was planning on spending the rest of his life with was cheating on him. Not just once, but three times in Ruth's home. And not just on the floor, but twice in their bed. The second time as Ruth walked in on them. And this was the man I decided to devote my life to. What the hell was wrong with me?

Feeling suddenly exhausted, Paige went upstairs and lay down on the bed. Falling into a light sleep she was again soon awoken by her overwrought mind; by the thoughts of cheating on George that had been going through her head a few minutes earlier. Decades later it was eating at her as it never had when it was relevant; over all those months when George was the clueless idiot. Staring at the ceiling, what should have been obvious decades ago suddenly dawned on her: that *she* had been the reason for Henry's divorce. There was always the excuse that their marriage had never been good, and that even if Paige hadn't emerged on the scene, it would still have been an inevitable matter of time before something else triggered it. And maybe that, by accepting Henry's reckless invitations to their home, she had been secretly hoping for the outcome that became reality. Paige never asked Henry if Ruth was out of town. She didn't give his wife a second thought, other than having the vague sense of satisfaction at slipping into Ruth's role in Henry's life and taking it from her. All she knew was that she was determined to possess Henry, and if she possessed him only for the time they were making love, that was at least some measure of possession. The inevitable effects would wreak their havoc. Henry would never be able to think of her the same way again. He would never again see her as just another patron at the club who had come to hear his trio; someone who would disappear from his mind when the night had ended. They had been intimate. She knew him as his wife did. *I am part of Henry's life now.* The inadequacies of his marriage to Ruth would become more jarring and intolerable for him as his mind became increasingly filled with thoughts of Paige. Yet, as long as he remained married to Ruth; as long as he went home to her every night, Henry would still belong to her and not to Paige. He would continue to elude her, just as he did whenever he casually checked his watch and stood up to leave the coat check during one of their conversations about music. Always just when it seemed to Paige that she was making an impression, he'd smile, even if she was in the middle of a sentence, say something like "back to work" and leave. Obsession is a warped lens through which love is mimicked by poison. It didn't matter whether Henry and Ruth were really so contemptuous of one another that they never slept together, which Paige could never be certain of. In her whipsawing imagination, it may well have been that their sex life was as tumultuous as their apparent disdain for each other. The warped lens of obsession produced feelings of mistrust that grew increasingly in Paige; the fear that, on any given night, Henry could be betraying her. That he might be unfaithful to Paige with his own wife.

Continuing a relationship with George as if nothing had changed was a terribly selfish thing to have done – leading him on that way; sleeping with him, at first to avoid being alone, then only counter feelings of betrayal at the notion that Henry might be sleeping with Ruth. Yet it never inoculated her from those restless, uneasy thoughts. It only produced a period of weeks-long non-participating passivity in which Paige felt a growing, physical repulsion to George; as if they were opposing ends of a magnet. That hurt George deeply. He could not understand it. And it continued until, finally, Henry moved out of the home he and Ruth had shared. It was at that point that Paige told George that their relationship was over. Paige was confined again to the tiny, dilapidated studio apartment she had paid for with money earned by giving piano lessons. The apartment George had tried his best to convince her to give up.

Sitting up in the bed she had shared with Henry, the realization set in that she would soon be forced back to the small Manhattan apartment and to her students. Never in her wildest dreams would it have occurred to her young self that, decades later, she would still be earning her living by giving piano lessons. The betrayal of the young girl she had once been saddened Paige. What would she have done with her life if George hadn't wanted to please her by bringing her to the club where she had set her eyes upon Henry? Henry, who so often threatened to kill himself when life didn't meet his expectations; threats that Paige now knew meant he had more contempt for himself than love for her. He thought nothing of frightening her with the idea of leaving her alone. In his spiteful way, he may have even enjoyed taunting her with it. Even after his tantrums abated, the thought of loneliness terrified her. Now it had come, as she had always known it would one day, in one way or another. Her loneliness would now need to be hacked away at, like a sculptor pecking away at a piece of stone, eventually unveiling something new, or at least normal, the way Paige's guilt at her affair with Henry was chiseled away at by repeated transgressions until it had become normal; or at least until she had become numb to it. Paige knew she would have to sell the house; that she could not work enough to afford to keep it indefinitely. The weight of all that entailed was at once debilitating and nerve-wracking. She had no idea what she would do with its contents. Unable to lie in bed any longer, she went downstairs to the sofa. She looked at the kitchen table. The same oak table, another flea market purchase, that had been in the very same place since shortly after moving in. Paige was pulled to it, compelled to run her fingertips over its surface. I should wax it. It's been so long and it looks so nice after it's been waxed. Memories attached to it began flooding her mind, beginning with the two of them wondering whether it would be too big for the room; estimating how many people could sit at it; hauling it home, a process that was at first a comedy, which devolved into short-tempered frustration, but finally ended with self-congratulation and a sense of accomplishment when she and Henry had finally set it down, acknowledging with relief that it was indeed perfect. In the present, Paige sat on one of the chairs – the one at the end of the table that she always sat on when they had friends over. Her parents never sat together at that table. The trip from Chicago was too daunting for her father. Her mother sat there not long after her father had died; quiet and distant, at times seemingly not knowing where she was. Her mother's hands resting on the table and Henry, sitting next to her, observing her bewilderment, clasping them in his, giving her comfort. Why couldn't I bring myself to do that? I knew at that moment I would regret not doing it. I didn't know that the regret would stay with me every day for the rest of my life. She was grateful to Henry, but ashamed and angry that she had not been the one to have done it; to have simply taken hold of her mother's hands, and to have been the one to receive the hesitating, sideways glance of appreciation that her mother had given Henry. Paige put her hand on the same spot on the table, over that same knot in the wood; the knot which all the grain detoured around, that she had noticed as the predominant feature of its surface from the first moment she saw the table, and muttered to herself, 'I'm so sorry. I love you, mom.' It took some time for her eyes to dry and for the sorrow to drift away. She could not bear to be in the presence of that memory any longer; the memory of a single moment she could never take back and make good. Paige diverted her attention to the raised counter in the open kitchen, preferring to remember how they used to turn it into a bar on occasion; how it became crowded with liquor bottles, an ice bucket, and, yes, that red, hand-cranked ice crusher. The ice crusher. She had completely forgotten about it. That thing was witness to so much fun; to so many good times. What on earth happened to it? It could not have been thrown away. I haven't seen it in years and years; it must still be here somewhere—up there, in one of the cabinets, I bet. Filled with hopeful anticipation, as if finding it would somehow turn back the clock to another time, Paige moved a chair over to the sink and stood on it, opening doors to the cabinets above, one after another; looking over and through all the various glasses, plates, casserole dishes, moving the chair to the next, cabinet, and the next, until—there it was in the back of one of them. It always seemed to be behind other things, even when it was used frequently. The act of standing on the chair, stretching to see to the back of the cabinet; spotting the deep-red form with its silver lid; moving out all of the things in front of it, other things meant for special occasions, which she had also not used in many, many years; feeling the ice crusher's smooth plastic form and unique weight in her hands as she pulled it toward her, clutching it against her chest as she carefully stepped off the chair and carried it to the countertop. The familiarity of the minor, long-ago ritual returned. She ran her index finger over the brand name, *Ice-O-Mat,* engraved in script on the silver metal lid, which she opened. Slowly cranking the handle, Paige watched the big metal teeth turn. She recalled inspecting its mechanism the same way, as a curious child would, when Henry first brought it out from the box of things he had been storing it in when they were preparing for their house-warming party. The fact that he had taken it with him when he moved out of Ruth's apartment created an allure for her back then; they, too, had used it while entertaining friends. Now it, like Henry, had become part of Paige's life. She went to the freezer, got a tray of ice cubes, and threw some in. Pressing gently on the lid and turning the handle, haltingly at first, then more smoothly as the ice offered less resistance, Paige once more heard the familiar sound of ice being crushed and dropping into the bucket inside. Those sensations from the past conjured scenes and faces from long ago that floated through her mind in a kaleidoscope. Brunches for which the kitchen table was used as a buffet; wooden folding chairs all about the living room; freewheeling dinner parties; the house filled with lots of musicians, always one or another taking a seat at the piano, playing just a few bars or an entire tune, often accompanied by others who had brought instruments with them; string instruments, wind instruments, horns of various kinds lying about the house, some in their battered cases, others not, at times so many that they had to be stepped around; the last guest to arrive always seemed to be greeted with the same four dramatic piano chords from Beethoven's Fifth as they walked through the front door: *Ba-ba-ba-baaa!* Always the same gag that never got old. Sometimes tipsy singalongs would occur spontaneously; the laughter, the swearing, the playfully lewd comments, cigarette smoke filling the place so that it seemed like a jazz cellar, escaping in clouds through the opened back door; Andy Lahr, the sax player, skinny and inebriated, bashfully confessing his love for Paige as he crushed ice in this very machine, right here on this very spot, and how funny and cute she had found him. All stopped decades ago; in the late 1980s, she'd guessed. It had been a generation since she last used the ice crusher. Most of those faces had long since passed away, or moved away; a couple wound up feuding with Henry, one over a not so funny or cute pass at Paige. A few she had not seen in many, many years had somehow heard of Henry's death and had contacted Paige, traveling long distances to attend his memorial service, looking much grayer, heavier, older, barely recognizable. She was grateful to them. Again in the present, Paige turned to the dining table. A shout from Henry invaded her mind: 'That woman's whole life is a primal cry for attention!' It was only three or four years ago that Paige had invited Lara Mowens from the city to dinner. Not a musician, but a fan from the hotel who became a friend, Paige had been spending quite a bit of time with Lara in Manhattan. Paige could see Lara in her mind, sitting in the room in the hotel while she played, in the place she so often sat, sometimes alone, often with someone she had brought with her, listening, talking discreetly, always introducing them to Paige during breaks or at the end of the evening as her 'dear friend,' as if to show that she knew *everyone* around town. Henry, who had met Lara only on a couple of occasions, had taken an instant disliking of her. 'The only thing that woman ever talks about is herself! How small is a person's life when the only thing she can talk about is herself?' He griped about her visit for days before it happened. 'That woman never has anything interesting to say. She's a complete nitwit!' 'Lara has plenty to say. And she's not a nitwit; she's a lawyer.' 'A lawyer? You think she's some kind of Perry Mason? She defends greasy spoons that get caught thieving wages from their employees! And she's never had an informed opinion in her life. Every time she opens her mouth it is just to be contrarian. That's her idea of feeling smart!' 'Henry, if that's the way you feel about it, then please go out for a few hours. There is no reason for you to hang around here.' 'I'm not going to let that lard-ass chase me out of my own home!' I thought you were just trying to limit my contact to other people, Henry. But you weren't. I know you weren't. The litany passed through Paige's head, confirming that, as with so many other things, his criticisms of Lara had indeed been correct: that she was not interested in the least in other people unless they could be used to inflate her own sense of self; that she talked constantly about things she had done to help others, but really only to show that she had done so because everything was about vanity with Lara. Often she misused words, once using 'penultimate' as a superlative while describing food at a certain restaurant in the presence of Henry, which caused him to so obviously roll his eyes that Paige felt on edge the entire time, worrying whether Henry would bring it back to bite. Other flashes of memory passed through Paige's mind: That dinner at home; Lara talking about how she offered to buy her new colorblind boyfriend a pair of color-correcting eyeglasses so he could see how beautiful her 'amazing green eyes' were, and how exasperated she was when he refused to let her; Henry piping up with a bit of scorn: 'Maybe if you were concerned about him being able to see the true colors of nature instead of just your eyes, he might have felt you wanted to do something for him and not you.' Lara then wondering whether her boyfriend was really worth her time anyway since he had no idea about the plight of the Rohingya in Myanmar; and how could someone like her possibly be with a man like that? Henry, who read constantly and was informed about the world, saying that what was happening in Myanmar was a horrible tragedy, but then rattling off many other humanitarian disasters that were happening simultaneously in other parts of the world, all of which Lara was so obviously clueless about that she changed the subject to having probably saved an elderly neighbor from dying in a fire by replacing her ancient toaster oven; Henry proudly announcing that he was suffering from a severe bout of constipation due to a new medication, and Lara to launching into a lecture about how important it was to drink more water to 'make it easier for the cilia in the bowels to move things along,' causing Henry to explode in ridicule that it was muscular contractions that moved things along, not fine hairs. 'Every high schooler knows that. How could an adult possibly think otherwise!'; a flustered Lara stammering that when she lived in Italy, an Italian doctor once told her that. 'Don't blame the Italians for your own ignorance!' Henry shouted before storming out of the room, 'I have nothing against know-it-alls who actually know something, but you're the dumbest know-it-all I've ever met!' Lara, whose face rarely showed any emotion, reacting as if she were watching it all on TV; Paige driving Lara to the train station for the ride back to the city with Lara saying that Henry should 'get help with his anger problem.' Paige took satisfaction in defending Henry by replying that Henry did not now and has never had an anger problem. Paige had to smile, recalling Lara calling the next day: Henry, seeing Lara's name on the caller I.D. sighing and mumbling, 'Why are people like that allowed to have phones?' then answering, telling her that, 'She's not here. No one is here . . . No, I'm not here either,' and hanging up. When was it? I can't remember exactly. Had to be one of the last times I saw her. Paige recalled the surge of hurt that passed through her as she recalled once asking Lara why she never shared any personal stories about her childhood with her. After all, Paige shared her deeply emotional recollections about her father. Lara's matter of fact answer, 'Because you're not important enough' left Paige stunned. Wait, you hardly ever gave me the chance to tell you about my father. Whenever I tried you interrupted me—once to talk baby talk to a dog on the street! God, Henry, you were so right. Why couldn't I see it? Why couldn't I see it when Lara brought me along to a party, and on the way began ridiculing the intelligence of the friends who had invited her? What kind of upbringing creates that kind of person? 'When someone announces over and over how horrible they are you should believe them,' she recalled Henry saying more than once. Paige realized that Henry was a much better judge of character than she was; that Lara indeed was, as Henry had always described her, 'utterly awful.' She felt the warmth she felt back then, when Henry said that she was far too talented and genuinely good person 'to be wasting even one minute on person like that. She's had a small life and is jealous of anyone who hasn't.' Henry you did care about me. Paige felt the stun of the hand falling inappropriately on her thigh and squeezing it. The periodic sexual harassment heaped on her by Gonzalo, a manager at the hotel. His image in her mind had become so grotesque over the years that she could no longer imagine what he actually looked like. His lewd innuendo, which Paige so often tolerated as raunchy humor, had gradually devolved into inappropriate touching. She had become adept at warding off unwanted advances, but this man was her boss; he was persistent and it continued every night until he finally backed Paige into a corner in a deserted room, pressed himself against her and let his hand run over her bottom. Paralyzed by shock and an unaccustomed fear, it took an indeterminate amount of time, feeling his hands running over her before she was able to summon the flash of energy necessary to pushed him away and flee. In her nearly two decades performing at the hotel, this was the only period she dreaded going to work. 'Paige, what's wrong? Why won't you tell me?' she heard Henry say. Paige thought she had been concealing it well, but Henry knew her better than anyone. Whether Lara, Paige, or anyone else, Henry was an astute observer of people with an uncanny ability to see right through them. The now inexplicable shame she felt back then kept Paige from telling him. Yet, Henry sensed what was happening, knowing it intuitively. As with a parent's greater experience over a child who thought she had the world figured out, Henry seemed to have been expecting this day would come and had prepared for it. Her reactions to his gentle questioning confirmed it for him. 'Who is doing this to you?' *Doing this to you.* Hearing that question pushed Paige to tears. Henry held her as she wept, haltingly telling him what was happening. Paige awoke feeling bone-weary;

the confession the previous night had taxed her to her soul. Henry had already showered and was getting dressed, 'I've got a few errands to run.' He returned hours later, never mentioning where he had gone. She felt nauseous during the commute to the city next afternoon, wondering what Gonzalo had in store for her. But from that day onward Gonzalo's harassment not only stopped, but he avoided Paige altogether, communicating with her only through other hotel employees, one of whom said, 'Your old man is one tough motherfucker.' It wasn't long before Gonzalo was gone altogether and a new manager was hired. Paige had not felt so loved and protected since she was a little girl in the days before her father had fallen ill when she found out that Henry, who could assume a scary, threatening persona when he wanted to, went that day to see Gonzalo personally. Henry never told her what he said or did that day, only mumbling, 'I thought it would,' when Paige told him the harassment had stopped. How effortlessly he had baited Lara with his constipation story; how selflessly he had stood up for her against the hotel manager. What a special man he was. 'Henry I miss you. How can I go on without you?' His permanent absence became more intense now, manifesting itself in increasing aching throughout her body, from her chest to her fingertips. She climbed the stairs to the bedroom, drawn to it almost reflexively; to be at the point of the greatest intimacy. She sat on the bed, running her hand over the sheets that she and Henry had slept on together. Yet, what came to mind was not passion, but the years throughout which she submitted to his usual advances at the usual time; his embrace from behind, how she responded mechanically, hoping only that he would be quick so she could sleep, and the silence that always followed. Paige wondered when their estrangement from passion began and who had been responsible for it. Perhaps it was enviable. But something in her refused to believe that. She used to wonder whether Henry was thinking about someone else while he had sex with her. Now Paige wondered who that might have been. Was it someone from his past? Someone he may have seen randomly on the street? If that was the case, maybe it was she who was to blame. There were times, from the very beginning of their lives together, when Paige could be very unfair to Henry, and she knew it. Early in their relationship Henry had mentioned in passing that there was a period when he frequented strip clubs with friends back in Chicago. That caused an inchoate sense of envy in Paige, who, for several years, was jealous of the experiences Henry had, but she had not. She badgered him to take her to one, just for fun. He refused, 'You're being silly, Paige.' She found that condescending and kept pushing him. When he finally relented, she was so appalled at what she had seen there: the sleazy, oily-faced men stuffing money into the panties and bras of pole dancers; the lewd drunkenness; the stifling cigar smoke making her queasy, that she castigated him harshly for taking her to that kind of establishment. When he defended himself, saying it was Paige who had insisted on going, she berated him even more for having ever frequented such sleaze joints in the first place. Paige felt her toes curl in her slippers, cringing at how unjust it was. She had simply wanted to know everything that Henry's greater age had allowed him to experience, not because she wanted to know more about him, but because she was jealous. Next to Henry's, there were times she felt her own life comparable to Lara's small life. It took some time for Paige to realize that when Lara constantly talked about herself, or ignored Paige and involved herself in conversations with complete strangers in the subway, or in a movie line, that it was a not so subtle way of showing contempt for Paige because she was envious of her. Paige realized, too, that her envy of Henry caused her to resent him; to distance herself from him at times like a jealous adolescent. If there was an event Henry was old enough to have experienced, but she was not, Paige would intentionally demonstrate a profound disinterest in it when Henry spoke about it. After Henry left Ruth, the interest bordering on obsession that Paige had exhibited about every aspect of their lives together evaporated so obviously that Henry no longer bothered mentioning anything about Ruth or their marriage. Now she could see that the effect of it all was simply to push Henry away. It then occurred to her that maybe Henry *had* really loved her. Why else would he have tolerated such behavior? Maybe the reality was that *she* didn't have any love for Henry. Perhaps it was all obsession; an obsession that had gone on so long that Paige had become too fearful or lazy to break away from Henry when the fixation itself was over. Paige thought about the diaries she had pulled out of the trunk in the attic. How hateful the words were that she had written. Just thinking about them produced memories so vivid it was as though she felt their touch upon her skin. A deep sense of repugnance pervaded the bedroom surrounding Paige. She felt her long relationship with Henry, the house, and everything in it had conspired to steal a life she could have had but did not. A life where she could have stayed close to her parents, had children, a husband who would love her always, and whom she could love in return. She might have even had the career as a classical pianist that she had dreamt of when she was young. Vivid lost memories of the adolescent daydreams she'd have while lying on her bed after school invaded her mind; visions that she'd have almost every day for a time in her young life: she would be giving a recital in Chicago's Orchestra Hall; the audience applauding, some cheering, while her parents beamed with pride from the front row. That could have happened. She'd had the talent and the drive. It was within reach, or at least a genuine possibility, at some point in her young life. When exactly did she let that dream go? When did she give up Orchestra Hall, a venue that overwhelmed her with joy the very first time her father had taken her there, for a jazz club; the grand stage for a smoke-filled room in which people often talked over the instruments in conversations that were inebriated and petty? How many of the lines in her face would have not have appeared without a lifetime of late nights in the smoky, alcohol-drenched environments of the jazz clubs? Concert halls were heavenly; pure and noble places filled with sophisticated audiences as decent as her parents. Of course there were also sophisticated connoisseurs of jazz, but she now saw the clubs as toxic environments; basements which people drifted into and staggered out of, like transients in a flophouse in need of a dingy bed and a cheap meal. No one would ever think of propositioning her in a concert hall. Oily, drunken men constantly did in the jazz clubs. For them, she was nothing more than a pole dancer in one of Henry's strip joints. Henry. If only I had never set my eyes on him! He did this. It was because of him, the power that he exerted over me back then; a power which she still could not explain, but Henry knew he had possessed. That single night George took her to a jazz club changed the course of her life; it led to her, at sixty-seven years of age, sitting alone on a sofa in a house she could no longer afford to keep, with the daylight fading, financial resources dwindling, and the burden of liabilities growing. How different it all could have been but for that one cursed night! Regret, shame and sorrow she felt for the way she had treated her father filled Paige. I could have stayed close to him. I could have made up for the selfishness I had displayed toward him when I was young and mean and clueless. In his presence, I would have grown older and wiser. Mom would not have been left struggling to care for him alone. I could have made money, who knows how much; possibly a lot of money. I might have had a recording contract. I could have cared for them both. I could have given them grandchildren who would have loved them; who would have brought joy to their lives. How wonderful of daddy to have brought me to Orchestra Hall. To have had the idea to surprise me with the tickets; to have gone out of his way to purchase them, standing in line at the box office, knowing, hoping that it would bring joy to his daughter. How lovely it must have been for him to have taken me to that place I had never even heard of before. He had done it out of pure love for me. I will never know that kind of joy. I will never know what it's like to want a beautiful life for my child. I rejected what that dear man tried to give me. What he worked hard to give to me. It seemed to her now that she rejected it out of pure spite, probably because he had gotten sick and become an emotional burden for her. Again, the tears of sorrow and regret poured from Paige's eyes. If only she could speak to her father one last time. Just the four words again passing through her lips and her heart: 'I love you, daddy!' If only I could make up for the way I treated you. Now it's too late for that. Now it's too late for everything. It's too late because of that fucking bastard I set my eyes on in the fucking smoky hellhole! Paige fell flat on the sofa and raged with her face against the cushion, 'I let myself be seduced by you, Henry! All for nothing good!'

. . .

Twilight had fallen upon the house; the time in the evening that Paige dreaded. The daylight fading to darkness made her surroundings, and life itself, seem surreal, empty, and set her vaguely on edge, pulling her deeper in the undertow of her thoughts; of her dulled and aching sensibility. Remaining stationary, she feared, would result in succumbing to it. She turned on the lights and went to the kitchen to prepare something to eat, more as a distraction than the need for food. Pulling away one moldy outer edge of one slice of white bread, she went to the refrigerator, grabbed a jar of peanut butter, opened it and smeared it over the bread with a knife taken from the sink. Chewing the gooey substance while leaning on the counter, she observed the piano. How different her life could have been if she had never learned to play it at all; if she had not fallen in love with it from the first touch of the keys. Her parents had surprised her with an upright for her eighth birthday. She found herself unable to stop touching the keys, experimenting with the sounds they produced, from that day onward. Until now.

Now, for the very first time since the day she had turned eight years old—nearly six decades—not only did the instrument hold no allure for her, she felt an inscrutable sense of queasiness and disgust at the sight of it. Before Henry, it had been the piano that had stolen her life. She had used it to shield herself from her father after he became incapacitated by his illness. Not only did nothing good come from her acquaintance with it, it had seduced her emotionally, just as Henry had done. With the queasiness and disgust giving way to rage, Paige impulsively flung the half-eaten slice of peanut-butter laden bread at the piano, hitting it. Stuck to its side, she watched as the bread slowly slid down the beautifully curved wood; curves that she had so often admired while sitting right where she was now. Her heart sank. That act of violence against the singular thing in her life that she had always unquestionably and genuinely loved caused her outburst of rage to melt into a pool of guilt and sorrow. A piano was given to her out of love by her parents. It was she who corrupted that love, using it not as an instrument of creative expression, but as a device to wall herself off from father. Just as she had perverted it by using it as a tool to impress Henry. That was all her doing. Suffering the grief over decisions that could never, ever be made right, Paige sobbed into her hands. Her face and palms, still wet with tears, and with the deference and love she had seen in her mother as she tended to her disabled father, she cleaned the piano, wiping away the streak of peanut butter, then rubbing its gentle curves, and the entire piano with furniture polish and a soft cloth. When it was done, she stood looking at her blurred, distorted reflection in its lacquered surface. There came the realization that it was no longer a piano. Never again would it be a musical instrument. Never again would she take pleasure or find pride in playing it. It was now simply a piece of furniture. An heirloom from a former life. 'Even this you took from me, you fucking bastard. Now I am nothing.'

What was that damned name?! she thought, turning away from the piano. It was a name that would have been fitting for a girl or a boy. Of course, it was connected to music; a musician's name. She knew it for decades after the abortion. Yet now her memory failed. How could a secret of such intimacy ever have been erased? She tried coaxing it from her mind with syllables, letters of the alphabet; she racked her brain with the names of jazz musicians, classical composers; it was a name, she recalled, that would be appropriate for a child but would seem more sophisticated with age. She tried to get it back, and at times she felt it was almost there; flashes of something in her mind that she could nearly grab onto, only to have it slip away. Paige felt as if her head was filled with a jelly that prevented the synapses in her brain from functioning, from connecting with one another. An inexplicable and sudden fear emerged; that the loss of the name would result in the loss of the child all over again. She could only hope that it would come back to her in time; that, as with so many other vanished thoughts, it would, out of nowhere, magically reappear once again in a flash, as if it had been there, safe all along. If it happened, she would write it down so that it could never be lost again. But the fact that it was gone now agitated her, ginning up even more hatred of Henry; Henry who had stolen two lives—hers and their baby's. The collision of just two cells would have unleashed an entire lifetime's worth of joy and pain. A history that would slowly unfold over decades, affecting an unknown number of other lives. Maybe a life of brilliance, or maybe Leopold Lojka, the man whom Henry was always so fascinated by; the Chauffeur whose wrong turn led to World War I and the suffering and deaths of millions. *Leopold Lojka. That name I am capable of remembering, but not the name I had given to my own child!* Henry did that, too. He was intrigued by that history, which meant it had to become stamped in my brain, too. And my child's gone. Fuck Leopold Lojka! My baby would have had musicality. My child would have been musically inclined. How could it not have been? It would have grown up surrounded by music. My child would have been a musician. How could it have possibly been otherwise? It had musical genes. But it didn't matter now. It didn't matter because it never was. It was nothing. Now we are both nothing. Nothing, and with no future. I have a rotten past and you none at all.

Paige heard the rain outside rising to crescendo and wondered how long it would last. Not that it mattered. She was staying in the house. She stared at the piano that was no longer a musical instrument. Now it is furniture. What can this piece of furniture be? It's a table. It has a large, flat surface. It can be nothing else. If there is ever again a time when people are gathered in the house, I'll use it as a buffet. This way the kitchen table would be free for people to eat at. A table needs an ornament. Something to give it purpose when it isn't being used. A bookshelf holds books. A table should always have something on it. It had been ages since she had been aware of holding the bronze candlestick now sitting on the bookshelf; of looking at it closely. Feeling it brought her instantly back to the very first time she had held it; the very first time she had picked it up, felt the weight of it and the curves of the cool brass in her hands. Some of the fingerprints she could see on it under the light were surely Henry's. Purchased long ago at one of their many outings to local flea markets, it had been in the house for decades. Paige thought that she could take the cloth she had used to clean the piano and wipe it clean of Henry's touch; another small step in banishing him from her life forever. Unlike his body itself, which had been reduced to carbon and released into the environment, into the Hudson River, the fingerprints, as if evidence of a crime, once erased, would simply vanish leaving no trace behind. Henry had encouraged her to buy it. He had stood, watching her admiring its unusual form; judging the weight of it in her hands. She had thought it unnecessary and too expensive. Henry reached into his pocket and, after a quick negotiation with the seller, bought it for her. 'If it makes you happy, then I'm happy' she remembered him saying, looking in her eyes with such love that it made her hostility toward Henry morph at once into a longing for him. Then, from deep in the recesses of her mind, the night at the club. The break between sets. Henry disappearing into the cloakroom. Paige discreetly following after a couple of minutes. He looked up from the book he was reading. He pulled her against him and started kissing her, which she willingly engaged in. It was the very first time. She felt Henry's hand slide down her hip and up her short skirt, then the pressure of his hands on her shoulders, pushing her down to her knees. He unzipped his pants. She was too stunned to move as he shoved himself inside her mouth, pushing her head against him. Quickly, over and over. The gagging on his pulsing discharge, not knowing what to do with it before ingesting him. Paige slowly stood up, staggered out of the coat-check room in a daze. My God, is Henry here? No, not Henry, I mean George. Is George watching me now? Please don't let him see me now. No, no, I came here alone, thank God. Wiping her mouth with the back of her hand, she went to the woman's room, retreating into the dirty stall and stood there heaving and shaking. You never apologized for what you did to me! You never once mentioned what you did to me! Humiliation and disgust invaded her senses and turned to rage. She stood up, trembling, needing to release her fury on something, not knowing what. Paige ran up the stairs to Henry's studio. She switched on the light. The anger and pain that she should have felt back then, when she was young, was now swelling inside her. The painting of the young girl on her knees mocking her. Henry, even in nothingness, mocking her. She grabbed the painting as if it was Henry by the throat and threw it violently against the wall, breaking its frame. Then stomping and kicking at it until the canvass was torn and mutilated;

until Henry's vision was unrecognizable and Paige exhausted. One last fit of fury upended Henry's brushes and oils from the small table next to the easel where he had last set them down, sending them all into the air and scattering on the floor. Paige fled the studio; stumbling down the stairs, she retreated to the sofa in the living room, falling into it, numb. Her anger was now futile. She had recognized it too late in life. I can do nothing to him now. Henry no longer exists. And what if I no longer existed? What's to fear from non-existence? I won't exist, and so what? No one will even notice I'm gone. It doesn't make one whit of difference to anyone whether I'm here or not. I don't want to live in this emotional pain and turmoil anymore. Life is done for me. I threw my life away and what is left now is irredeemable. There is nothing to look forward to. Only scrambling for a living, selling the house, and what am I ever going to do with the accumulated lifetime of things sitting in it? If only she could just walk away from it all. Just leave this house and never return to it. Abandon it to thieves. To the elements. The roof needed work. The rain now pouring down upon it was probably already leaking in somewhere above her head. It would be the first to rot; the first to collapse, pulled down by the force of gravity, just as it had pulled the peanut butter slice to the floor. Weather would take care of everything else in it, including the piano, slowly erasing it all until any trace of her life with Henry would eventually turn to nothingness, like shipwreck slowly dissolving on the ocean floor; just as was happening to Henry's pile of carbon at the bottom of the Hudson River. Let it all just wither away like an ancient ruin with a 'condemned' sign on the front door. By order of Duchess County this property is hereby *condemned*. By order of my own fucking stupidity, my life is hereby *condemned*. It was condemned the moment I laid my eyes on that fucking bastard. What does it matter now? In a few years anyone who knew us will also be gone. There will be nothing left. Not even a memory. Nothing. It will be as if we had never existed. Failure, everything's a fucking failure. The world itself was a fucking mess. Let the whole thing burn, I couldn't care less. She asked herself a terrible question over and over: whether it was all worth it. And each time the equally terrible answer came that it was not. Darkness now enveloped the house accompanied by the rain. It was the time in the evening that had sent a nebulous sense of anguish and panic running through her since Henry had died. Even before he had died, when he was so sick and she knew the time was quickly approaching when she would be sitting there alone, the darkness could spark an anxiety attack in her. Paige recalled holding Henry's hand as his life slipped away. At that moment tears flowed from his eyes. 'I had the stupid feeling that you were crying because you had to leave me. But you were crying for yourself, you selfish son of a bitch! You miserable, rancid prick!' Paige laid her head down on the sofa and began weeping uncontrollably, shouting into the cushion, 'You fucking bastard! I hate you! I hate you! You ruined my life!' she shouted that over and over. 'I loathe you! I have nothing but contempt for you!' She raged on that way, angry with herself for not knowing words that could adequately express the true depth of her hatred for him, shouting into the sofa cushion until physically and emotionally exhausted by it. There won't be anyone to hold my hand when I die.

She wouldn't go to bed. The act of picking herself up off the sofa and walking up the stairs would begin the process of her brain becoming active, resulting in her experiencing the turmoil of emotions she had lived and relived every day since Henry had died, causing her insomnia to return. 'You ruined my life. I am nothing. This is how you left me. I am *nothing!*' Why do people so greedily cling to life, even when they are in immense pain? Even when they know all is hopeless? Because they are greedy. I am not greedy. I am nothing. What difference does it make whether I am dead or alive? Either way I am nothing. At least in death the nothingness would be painless. I wouldn't have to live with the pain I feel every single day I keep myself alive; with the permanent regret of a life wasted on that motherfucker. I *wasted* my life. People who lead frivolous lives at least can say they had a good time. I can't even say that I enjoyed what I lived. What I had always thought was important turned out to be garbage. Regret is all that is left. I hate my life. I *hate it. Please*, just let me die tonight! Just let me die here and rot in this fucking house! I don't deserve anything else! Again, her rage poured into the sofa cushion, now with the same voracious intensity with which the rain was pounding the house. She pressed her face harder against the cushion as she raged even more into it, *I hate my life!* she managed to shout, squeezing it out along with the last of the breath still in her lungs, then, yet another, weaker push, straining, seemingly out of a chest already emptied, a last cry conjured of pure loathing, from a face flushed, lacking oxygen, as if possessed: *I hate my life. . . Let me die!* Paige refused to draw a breath, determined to suffocate herself, squeezing her chest further, holding the contraction, then finding the strength squeeze even more, now from her abdomen, wheezing overshadowed by the winds whipping around the house; refusing to let herself inhale, holding and squeezing only emptiness while the rain pounded and the spirits howled, mocking the living, contracting muscles tightening around her pounding heart, her face burning with redness, with an anger intent on extinguishing her life.

A dreamless, mystical trance, during which she might have heard the telephone ringing;

the recorded message on the answering machine switched on: 'Leave *us* a message.' '*Fuck you,*' she said, throat sore from her loathing, falling back into dazed sleep. Then, at some indeterminate time, not knowing exactly where she was, or whether she was asleep or awake, Paige distinctly heard her father's voice, 'Where are my girls! We love you, Paige. You know we've always loved you. I've always loved you.' Her eyes sprang open, heart skipping a beat, then pounding hard in her chest, *"Daddy?!"* She lifted her heavy head from the sofa cushion. The house was filled with daylight. Paige slowly sat up, her body leaden, as if she had drunk too much alcohol the night before, yet with a nervousness in the center of her chest. She tried processing what she had heard so distinctly. There was no doubt in her mind that it was indeed her father's voice. He had come to her. He had come to comfort her. To ease her suffering. In a strong voice she said, 'Daddy, I love you and mommy both!' and began sobbing so uncontrollably, she didn't know whether it was possible to stop. She had no desire to. She wept until it simply wasn't possible anymore. Until there were no tears left. Then she simply sat, observing the house, fixing her presence in it. Finally, she stood up and went to the kitchen where she discovered that it was nearly ten o'clock in the morning. Paige could not remember the last time she slept in. Not until ten. Needing to get the grogginess out of her head, she managed to find just enough coffee to make a pot. Waiting for the coffeemaker to finish brewing, she opened the door to the back porch. The yard was soaked from the storm, but drenched in sunlight. The chilly morning air flowed through the screen door, slowly erasing the last of the grogginess from her head. She stood there until she realized that the coffee maker had stopped percolating. Pouring herself a mug full, she saw there was a message on the answering machine attached to the kitchen wall. She pressed the 'play' button. She heard the familiar voice, George Haskell's voice, urgent and sincere. He had been away, staying with his son, daughter-in-law, and their family in Arizona. Only now had he heard about Henry's death. He was sorry, he said. He had always liked Henry. 'Please call me when you can, Paige. It's been too long. I want to know how you are. I know what you are going through right now. Please call me. You are still important to me, Paige. I care about you. I always have cared about you.' She replayed the message. It was good to hear the kind voice; a voice from a past which had not been burned to the ground. A past which, somehow, George would not let be torched and burned to nothingness. A past for which redemption was still possible. To hear the genuine concern he had for her again caused tears to well in her eyes. He still cared about her. After all the years, and all the callous disregard, he was still there for her. She felt freed from the bitterness and resentment of the previous night. She observed the piano, staring at it, contemplating it with the coffee mug warming her hands, recalling those first lessons. Walking the six blocks to the piano teacher's house. To Mrs. Natley's prim and perfect house filled with senseless knickknacks and her evidently expensive eight dollars an hour lessons. Six blocks with steps quick and measured, as if by a metronome, and full of purpose, ready to prove how hard she had worked to master the previous lesson and eager to move onto the next. Three years later, Mrs. Natley told Paige that she had advanced to the point where she needed to find a new teacher. She had begun with *Twinkle Twinkle Little Star* and was by then playing a perfect rendition of Satie's *Gnossiennes no. 1* without needing to look at the music. It was time for someone who could bring her further than her first teacher could. Paige recalled feeling that she might have worked too hard. She remembered how sad she felt at having to leave Mrs. Natley after what seemed like a lifetime. Eight dollars. What an odd amount, she thought. A far cry from the one hundred and twenty dollars Paige charged her students' wealthy parents in the city, a sum they never even flinched at. Nor did her older students: Lawrence Harvey, Bob Sims, Ed Stickyen. All successful, professional men who in retirement had decided the time had finally come to pursue what they had always loved. Larry was gifted. He could have been a concert pianist if he had started as a child. Bob and Ed were terrible, but she enjoyed teaching them because they were witty, intelligent, loved music and loved learning. More than many of her younger students did. They had all expressed their sincere condolences when Henry died. All were waiting patiently for her to return. To move on from her mourning. Larry, Bob and Ed would wait forever. They loved her. They had become part of her social life to varying degrees. The parents of the younger ones would only wait so long before finding someone new to teach their kids. None would ever outgrow her, but she wondered if any would miss her the way she had missed Mrs. Natley. She was certain they would all remember her, even decades from now. Some would give it up, but they would all know how to play. They would use what she taught them to show off at parties, or to impress a beau. There were a couple she was sure would go on to study music at a conservatory. They would remember her. She again realized they all existed. That she missed them. There was a world waiting for her; a world that was alive and was waiting for her to take a part in it once more.

With the excuse that it was too wet to go out and sit on the porch, Paige took the coffee to the piano, not even realizing that she hadn't added milk. She sat down, set aside the coffee mug, lifted the fallboard and spread her fingers over the keys. She pressed a key. F sharp. She pressed another key. Then another just at random; just to hear the sounds in no particular pattern. She wasn't put off by what she heard. The patterns then became a few bars of *Twinkle Twinkle Little Star*. Paige felt herself smile. On to Gershwin's *Rhapsody in Blue*, which always delighted her father, 'Do you remember this, Daddy?' Moving with the music, onto numbers from the Great American Song Book, one merging into another, then to more complex compositions: Chopin, Mozart, Rachmaninoff, each with more confidence, flowing into the next, finger movements growing more familiar, more fluid. Paige was fully enjoying herself, the sounds becoming louder until the melodies reverberated around the house, filling it with life, like a benediction from the heavens finding its true expression through her hands. As she played, she could hear Henry inside her head: 'Get on with it, Paige. *Get on with it!*'